Love Affair

Love Affair

Copyright © 2018 by Melanie Krystal

No part of this publication may be reproduced, distributed, or transmitted in any form or by any means, including photocopying, recording, or other electronic or mechanical methods, without the prior written permission of the author, except in the case of brief quotations embodied in critical reviews and certain other non-commercial uses permitted by copyright law.

Tellwell Talent

www.tellwell.ca

ISBN

978-1-77370-451-7 (Paperback)

By MELANIE KRYSTAL

For my Husband, Randy Parker,
Who made me believe in True Love

For my Nana, Shirley Baker,
Who showed me that with strength and
dedication anything can be accomplished

<h1 style="text-align:center">Prologue</h1>

The first day of school was always the hardest, even when you started with everyone else. However, it was even harder when you started in the middle of the school year when everyone else was starting their second term. My parents had just moved to a new city because my father, a journalist, had just got a new job at the paper

We had always lived in small towns, but now we were living in a big city. It was a huge adjustment for me. Where I came from, everyone knew everyone else. I never worried about strangers. I never worried about walking down the street alone. I usually hung out at the library where the librarians knew me so well that they knew what books I would want and would have a stack ready for me when I arrived.

I was only twelve, and all I ever wanted to do was to read my books. I could never get enough stories to fill my imagination. I loved to enter alternate universes; they were always better than the dull one I thought I lived in. I always carried a book, so that I could read whenever I wanted to.

So, it was no surprise that I was reading a book under an oak tree at the back of the school field when other kids from my new school decided to come over and talk to me. They thought I was reading because I needed to do extra studying. What they didn't know was that I was already ahead of the entire class.

"Hey, look, the new girl is so stupid, she has to read during recess to figure out what the teacher is going to talk about," Josh, a school jock, said as he pointed and laughed. They had been playing soccer, and the ball had come close to me. Josh crossed his arms and put his foot on the ball. His friends came up beside him.

"Hey, Stupid. What are you reading about?" Michael, Josh's friend, said. Everybody was laughing. I felt the tears pooling behind my eyes. These kids weren't like the kids from my last school. I never got made fun of for reading at my old school. It wasn't fair that the kids at my new school were so cruel while the kids at my last school usually just left me to my books.

"I'm not stupid. I like to read …" I mumbled. Just then, a group of girls from my class walked up to see what the boys were laughing at. They studied the dress my mother had made me and then my chipped fingernails. They wore designer outfits and makeup, and their nails were painted to match their clothes. It seemed as if all their parents had enough money to buy them whatever they wanted.

"Look, she isn't even smart enough to dress herself better. She probably got her dress out of a dumpster," Kylie said.

"Yeah, and she doesn't even know what nail-polish is. What is this world coming to?" Kylie's friend Jolene piped up.

"My mom made me this dress. I thought it looked like Wendy's dress from *The Wizard of Oz*," I mumbled. Another boy now stood with everyone else who was laughing at me.

"Yeah, sure, well, if that's what Wendy's dress looked like, she must have been a loser, too," Josh said.

"Poor, stupid bookworm," Kylie and her friends taunted. My cheeks heated up, and my eyes started to spill over. I wiped away my tears with the sleeve of my sweater.

"She likes books, and she loves her parents, I don't see anything wrong with that," the new boy said as he sat down next to me. "Why don't you all just mind your own business and leave her to her books."

"Why should we, Alexi? Are you going to go tell the teacher on us?" Josh taunted as the teacher started walking in our direction. "Whatever, she's not worth a detention," he said, and then he grabbed his ball and left with his friends.

It wasn't until everyone else left that I noticed that Alexi was still sitting beside me. He had pulled out a batman comic book and was avidly reading. He glanced up from his comic and smiled as he caught me looking at him. I knew at that moment that we were going to be great friends.

Chapter One

"So, you're really going to be Kalea's man of honour for her wedding?" Julius asked as we returned to his apartment after playing three rounds of one-on-one. I tossed the basketball back into his closet and then flopped down onto his couch.

"Yeah, why wouldn't I want to be her man of honour? It's not like she has many girlfriends she's that close to, other than Candace, of course, but even Candace doesn't know her like I do," I said.

Julius tossed me a bottle of water. "You don't think that's going to be weird? Standing beside her as she vows to be faithful to another man?"

"Why would it be weird? It's not like I'm in love with her. She's my best friend and I'm happy for her."

"Uh huh, you seem to forget that I've seen the two of you together. You're made for each other. Hell, you don't even have to speak most of the time; you both know what the other's going to say before they even say it."

"I'm not into Kalea! She's like a sister to me, and we've been friends since we were twelve! She's in love with Charles, and that's who she belongs with," I shrieked.

Julius popped in a movie. "I'm just saying. It's weird that it's not the two of you getting married. If you weren't so scared of your feelings, maybe it would be."

"Drop it, man. I'm not in love with Kalea," I said. I got up and grabbed a beer out of his fridge.

"See, look! You even need a drink just thinking about Kalea getting married to someone else. Why don't you just tell her how you feel, man?"

"I don't tell her I feel that way, because I don't feel that way, Julius. Now drop it before I beat the crap out of you."

"Whatever you say, man. But we both know the truth. You love her, you're just too scared to admit it."

"You don't know anything. I'm not in love with Kalea. I know what love is, and this is definitely not it."

"You're saying what you had with Drea was love?"

"Yeah, it was. Until, of course, she got tempted. That's when the relationship fell apart. We would have lasted forever if she hadn't done what she did."

"You mean, the temptations of sleeping with other men? Cause trust me, if what you had with Drea is love, we're all doomed."

"Shut up and turn on the game. We already missed the first half," I said. He shook his head. I knew that what I had with Drea wasn't love in the end. But in the beginning? It certainly was.

She completed me. She made me feel like everything would work out in the end, even if everything was falling apart. My mom hated her guts from the beginning. So, did Julius and Kalea for that matter. My mom, just like them, always thought that there was something wrong with her.

What I felt for Kalea was completely different. What an outrageous idea! It couldn't be love. Julius and I watched the game in silence as I pondered: what did I feel for Kalea? Sure, we were close, but who wouldn't be considering how long we'd been friends?

WEDDING PLANNING WAS TAKING FOREVER. Everything needed a decision. It was a shame my mom wasn't here to help with all the plans, flowers, cake flavours, and dresses, and so on. Luckily, Alexi was meeting me to help me figure out what to do for wedding favours. Charles and I were only having a small wedding, but I still wanted something that guests could use afterwards.

Choosing Alexi as my man of honour was the best decision I had ever made. He always chooses things that go perfect together, and he had the same vision for my wedding as I did. Candace was my bridesmaid, but she didn't even live in the same city as I did. She was in New Zealand for school. It had always been our dream to study literature in New Zealand, and I would have gone with her, but Charles said long distance relationships never worked out. I had applied anyways to see if I could get in and when my acceptance letter came I was thrilled. But I knew how Charles felt. He didn't want me half way around the world. So, the letter went into the bottom of my desk drawer. I really wanted to go but it would mean having to leave Charles behind. We had our differences and he got on my nerves sometimes, but I had been with him for seven years. I loved him, but I was starting to think I was making a mistake. Marrying someone was a life-altering decision, and I really didn't want to spend my life with someone I didn't belong with.

"You look like you're worried about something. I sure hope it isn't the wedding favours, because we're about to fix that problem. There has to be something in this giant department store that will work," Alexi said as he came up behind me. Of course, he was ten minutes late, but that was to be expected. He was never on time. Not once in all the years I'd known him. It was as if his internal clock was set a couple hours behind everyone else's.

"I was contemplating whether I'm making a mistake. I don't want to end up marrying the wrong person," I said as we went inside to start the hunt for wedding favours.

"Well, cold feet are natural, but I don't think you're making a mistake."

"Uh huh, I'm glad you're so certain about this."

"I'm completely certain. You two are meant for each other. I know that just by watching your eyes light up when you talk about him. And by the way you two look at each other. Yup, there's never been a doubt in my mind that you're marrying the right person."

"But …"

"No buts. Now, wedding favours! Do we want them to go with the colour scheme of the wedding? Cause candles would be an awesome choice, but do you want the same colour of candle for each guest? How many people are coming again?" he asked. We were in an aisle that was filled with all sorts of candles.

"There's a total of thirty-two people coming out of the forty that were invited," I said as I followed him.

"Candles seem so ordinary, though, don't they? Oh, what about little birdcages filled with treats or something? Maybe mints, cause then you could have a sign that says something like: *Mint to Be.*"

"Candles are pretty ordinary, but, then again, everyone could use them. I don't want to give out candy as a wedding favour. What else could we fill the birdcages with? They sound cute. Where in the world did you go?"

"I'm over here, towards the book section. They're really neat." he said, holding up a tiny black antique-looking bird cage for my inspection.

"It's absolutely adorable. We could put something like a washcloth inside or maybe a tiny candle."

"You really want to give out washcloths at your wedding? That's slightly mundane, don't you think?" he said, eyebrows raised.

"I guess not, but what else could we put inside? Let's keep looking. I want these bird cages, but we need something to go in them."

"You're the boss … I mean, bride."

"I still don't know if I'm making the right decision or not. What if he changes? What if I change? What if I lose who I am? You know I got accepted to the University of Canterbury, right? To study literature with Candace."

"What? Really?"

"Yeah. I hid my acceptance letter though. It would be a dream come true to go study with Candace. But with Charles and the wedding…"

"Kalea, if you want to go then he can't stop you from going."

"I know. I love him, I do. At least I think I do. I'm just nervous. What if everything changes once were married? What if I'm supposed to go to New Zealand to find my true love? What if…"

"What if a hurricane comes and kills him? What if you drown during your honeymoon? What if you both get struck by lightning and lose your memories? There's a ton of 'what ifs' in the world; you can't worry over every little one."

"I guess so but …"

"Kalea! Stop it!" he said. He held my shoulders and looked into my eyes. "Do you love him?"

"It's not that simple, Alexi."

"Yes, Kalea, it is that simple." He sighed. "If you're completely positive that Charles is the one you love, the one you're *in* love with, then you're making the right decision. Nothing else matters. If you both are in love with each other, you'll be happily married and spend many years with each other. Now, can we pick out your wedding favours without your cold feet getting in the way?"

"I guess so … Thank you, Alexi."

"What about flower seeds? Like a small burlap pack of tulip seeds or, wait, even better, a small burlap-wrapped tulip bulb that your guests can plant in the ground, and if the flowers grow, so does your love."

"That's actually really sweet. What a great idea. We could put the bulbs inside the birdcages to go with the theme of the wedding. I knew there was a good reason that I picked you for my man of honour."

"Exactly, you grab thirty-two tulip bulbs and I'll head back and pick up the bird cages. We can meet up at the till."

"Okay, sounds like a plan, see you in a few minutes."

Chapter Two

The stones of the castle wall were a light tan colour which brought out the colour of the giant purple ribbons streaming from the turrets. The patio was made of stone and the fountain where the angel poured water from an urn was magnificent. The patio was surrounded by beautiful green gardens with flowers of all colors. There were trees surrounding the lawns and four magnificent stone towers arching over the whole grounds.

The chairs for the guests were already set up with blue ribbons on the lawn where the ceremony was taking place. The stone patio was dressed up with purple and blue ribbons, and flowers for the cocktail hour. The reception was taking place in the grand ballroom with giant windows that looked out over the gardens. It was a venue fit for a princess.

It was a few minutes before the ceremony began. I felt so nervous, like butterflies were continuously fluttering their little wings inside my stomach. It felt like I couldn't breathe. My dress felt like it weighed a thousand pounds; I couldn't stop sweating. I really hoped nobody noticed.

"You ready, Princess?" I shook myself and grabbed my purple-and-blue bouquet from the table before turning towards my always-happy father. His smile and jokes were the stuff of legends. It was what made his column such a hit in the newspaper.

"I guess so, Dad. A little nervous, but I guess I'm ready."

"You look beautiful, Princess. Don't let anyone tell you otherwise," he said as he took my arm and led me outside to where the ceremony was going to take place.

The sun shone through the towers and brought out all the colors of the beautiful blue ribbons on the guests' white chairs. Purple pomander balls and Chinese lanterns hung from trees around us. The beautiful arch that Alexi and I had woven with flowers stood behind the Justice and Charles. Alexi was already standing in place, wearing a grey tuxedo with a purple tie and vest. By his side was Candace in her beautiful purple dress.

Charles and his two friends were standing opposite Alexi and Candace in their black tuxedos with blue ties and vests. I could remember the first time I saw Charles. It had been in tenth grade. My teacher had handed back our midterm tests in math class. I hadn't done very well, so I went to the tutoring centre and there was Charles. I had heard a lot about him because he had broken the heart of one of my classmates.

I had heard that he was jerk and that he treated women as if he owned them. But when I saw him, I was overwhelmed with how handsome he was. I ignored all the warnings that I had heard throughout the school and signed up for him to be my math tutor.

A few months later, he had asked me out and it had gone from there. I could still remember how he had treated me when we first started dating, he would carry my books and open doors for me. He had even filled my locker with lilies on my birthday. The music started bringing me back to the present, sending more butterflies to flutter in my stomach. My father slowly led me down the aisle. I stared at Alexi with everything I had. He knew I wasn't making a mistake, and I needed his words to come back to me.

If you are completely positive that Charles is the one you love, the one you're in love with, you are making the right decision. Nothing else matters. If you both are in love with each other, you'll be happily married and spend many years with each other.

Finally, I looked in the eyes of my groom. He was smiling, but he seemed more scared than happy. It felt like eternity passed while we exchanged vows and rings. Finally, the ceremony was over. Charles and I walked hand-in-hand back down the aisle towards the other side of the yard. We were followed by our bridal party. The guests were ushered over to the food and drinks that were set up on the patio for cocktail hour while we went to get our pictures taken.

Photo after photo was taken to capture the memory of our union. It didn't feel like we had gotten married, though. I was relieved that the ceremony was over more than anything else. I should have felt more than relief about my wedding.

Was the wedding planning that much of a burden? Or was I making the biggest mistake of my life?

I was glad everyone around me seemed so happy about the wedding, though I couldn't shake the feeling in my gut that I had just signed my life away. It felt like a death sentence had been passed on me.

I STOOD AT THE LEFT-HAND side of the flower covered arch watching as Kalea came down the aisle with her arm linked her dad's. Kalea looked so beautiful in her white, strapless floor-length wedding gown that it took most of my strength to keep myself where I belonged. I needed to stay as far away as possible from her. I hadn't really thought what Julius had said was true but, then again, I was an idiot when it came to my feelings.

As I looked into her deep, almond-shaped eyes I felt my heart slowly stop beating. I watched in agony as she married Charles. It felt like a knife was being plunged into the deep parts of my chest. It was excruciating to think that, even given how long we'd known each other, I couldn't tell her the truth of my feelings.

It seemed like centuries passed until we were all ushered into the grand ballroom of the castle for the reception. The gold tapestries on the wall worked wonders with the shades of blue and purple that decorated the room. Balloons with lights inside them floated along the edge of the dance floor. The smell of the roast chicken and asparagus wafted in from the kitchen and made my mouth start watering.

"You're so pale; it looks like you don't have any blood left in your body," Julius said, shaking me out of my thoughts of dinner. My stomach wanted food, but I also felt nauseous. Truthfully, it made me sick to my stomach to realize that Kalea was married.

"There you are. I was starting to think you ditched me for Candace. I know you have a crush on her," I said as Julius strode up beside me.

"I thought about it, but Kalea would kill me if I slept with her best friend … again." He winked as we headed over to our table. Kalea had it set-up so that the bride, the groom, the bridal party and their guests were all seated at the same table.

I didn't have an actual date for the wedding, and so I had brought Julius along. I was hoping now that he would be able to keep my head off Kalea and her beauty while this whole thing played out. I really didn't want to ruin her perfect day. I wanted her wedding to be everything she had ever wanted.

Already sitting at the table were Charles' two friends and their two dates, who were dressed in velvet skirts and blouses that barely contained their chests. Josh had his head down, as if he was in a lot of pain. It serves him right. He was a jackass. I hadn't liked him since that day he picked on Kalea for simply reading a book. The day we met was branded in my mind, and since that day I had always been protective of her.

It took all my strength to curb my desire to throttle him. It made no sense in the world why Kalea had allowed Charles to choose Josh as his best man after what Josh had put her through in school. Did Charles even know? He had only met Josh in college when they were both business majors. They were now business partners in a small marketing company.

Gregory, Charles' other low-life friend, was talking to both his own and Josh's dates about cars. He was talking so fast though; I'm surprised the ladies were still listening to him. He was an accountant, and he had been friends with Charles for almost as long as I had been friends with Kalea.

"I know you're the man of honour and all, but I totally want to sit beside the bride. I never get to see her anymore. You get to see her all the time," Candace said as she came up from behind us and sat down in the seat with my name on it.

"Whatever you want. Didn't you bring a date?" I asked, having noticed there wasn't a place setting for her guest.

"I was hoping you'd bring Julius and I'd be able to steal him for most of the night. Besides Brad couldn't make it. He said he was sick." Brad was Candace's new boyfriend from what I had heard. I also knew he wasn't sick. Kalea had mentioned that Brad and Candace weren't currently getting along and that I shouldn't bring him up to Candace. Kalea hadn't wanted to upset Candace at her wedding.

"He didn't bring me. I came on my own as a friend who wanted to help a friend," Julius said, immediately trapped in the confines of Candace's bright-green eyes. He took his seat beside her, and they were soon lost in conversation.

"Do either of you want a drink?"

"Sure, why not? I'll take a beer. Candace? How about you?" Julius asked without even looking in my direction. He was completely lost to her. He thought Kalea and I belonged together, but he hadn't watched as he flirted with Candace. He hadn't seen how she flirted in return and how they looked at one another.

When they finally hooked up a few years ago, Kalea and I had thought they would be together for good. But then Candace had gone off to New Zealand for school and that seemed to be the end of that.

"No, thanks. I have water and I have to drive tonight."

I left the two of them to talk as I headed over to the bar. I needed a drink. I needed Julius to keep my head in the game, but it seemed as if Candace was going to steal him away from me for the night. So, I grabbed a beer, chugged it down and ordered two more. Slowly I made my way back to the table where Julius was holding hands with Candace.

"Is anyone else starving? The photos and ceremony seemed to take forever," Kalea said as she arrived at the table with her groom in tow.

"Oh, girl, I am. But, then again, I'm always hungry," Candace said.

"I could eat," Julius agreed as he took his beer from my hand, and the bride and groom took their seats.

"Well, then, let's get this dinner served," Kalea said. She stood up to talk to the waiter.

"I'll get it, you just sat down," I said. "You need to relax. It's your wedding day, it's your day to be served." I put my beer down and headed off to find the person in charge. It didn't take me long to locate them and tell them that the bride wanted dinner served. I went back to the bar to grab myself something stronger than beer. I ordered two shots of whiskey, drank them quick and headed back over to the table.

Everyone except Charles was laughing. He looked con-stipated. Like he didn't want to be here. I felt my temper pulsing just below the surface. How dare he marry the great-est woman in the world, and not give a damn about how he treated her!

He looked in my direction and quickly changed his expres-sion and then tried to pretend he was part of the conversation. Still glaring at Charles, I sat down at the table next to Julius.

It didn't take long for the food to be served—the reception to be underway.

It seemed like a lifetime passed before the reception was finally over. I had spent most of the night around the bar trying to drink down the remnants of my love for Kalea. How could I have been so stupid? Why couldn't I have just acknowledged that I was in love with her when we were in school? Why couldn't I have turned down her offer of being her man of honour? Well, I knew the answer to most of those questions. Acknowledging my love would have led to me telling her I loved her, and that might have led to her rejecting me. And that? That was more than I could bear. I would do anything for her, including being the man of honour, even though it nearly killed me to do so.

"Hey, buddy, there you are." Julius said. "I was starting to think you left me so I could go home with Candace. Kind of hoped for that also, but I didn't want to leave with her in case you didn't make it home."

"Yeah. I thought about it, but I can't drive and I need a pad to crash at," I stammered. It was taking all my strength not to pass out.

"Geez, you look like crap. And you smell like a distillery. Didn't you stop drinking at all tonight?"

"I did actually, just now."

Luckily, Julius was sober. He had only had the one beer all night. He got me to his car and helped me back to his apartment.

"I love her, Julius; how could I be so stupid? I should have told her. I should have objected," I said as he helped me onto his couch.

"You couldn't, and you knew it. You knew that she would have not married Charles and instead you guys would be together. Ruining her wedding was the last thing you wanted to do, because you can't stand to see her unhappy," Julius said. He yanked off my shoes and tie. He then added: "Oh, and I told you so."

Chapter Three

Our flight to the Bahamas was over in the blink of an eye. It was probably because I had slept for most of it. The second we got off the plane, I was awed by the bright sun and the blue of the nearby ocean. The crispness of the sand against the water was breathtaking.

"Our hotel is this way," Charles said and headed in the direction of the beach.

"Yeah, it should be right on the beach."

"We should probably get checked in, and then we can change and go for dinner."

"That sounds nice. Are you tired? Or did you sleep on the plane?"

"I didn't get to sleep on the plane. You know I can't sleep on moving vehicles. I'm terrified of heights. There was no way I was sleeping on that plane."

"Maybe you should grab a nap before we go for dinner."

"Nah, I'll be fine. Besides, I'm excited to see that great, little family restaurant that I looked up online."

"Whatever you say, Charles," I said as I followed him.

We checked into our hotel and got changed before we rented a car from the hotel and headed to the restaurant. It was called Aloha, and it wasn't far from our hotel. It was a small log-cabin-type building right on the beach. There was a campfire with tables around it. It was beautiful.

We grabbed a table between the campfire and the beach so we could have the beach feel. I had loved the ocean since I was a little girl. My mom had loved it, too, and she used to bring me to the beach whenever she had the chance. She loved swimming, but she loved floating in salt water the best. She always said that people floated better in salt water and that floating was the most relaxing thing in the world.

The food at Aloha was amazing. We went straight back to our hotel once we were finished though. Charles was exhausted and needed to get to sleep. I wasn't tired in the least, and so I decided to go for a swim in the ocean.

I swam and floated for about an hour before I went back to the hotel. I climbed into bed beside Charles and stared up at the ceiling. It took a while, but eventually I slept.

The next morning Charles woke up with a bad stomach bug. He wasn't even able to keep down water. He told me to go do what we had planned to do that day.

I took the car and went horseback riding. The lovely sandy beaches were perfect for the horses. I spent hours riding with a mare named Georgia. When I was done, I called Charles to see if he was up for going for lunch. It was supposed to be our honeymoon, after all. He said that he hadn't been able to leave the bathroom since I left.

I told him that I would bring him some chicken soup, but he told me that he was fine. We had planned to go swimming with dolphins at 4 o'clock, but I was starving and I needed something to eat before dinner.

After parking the car in the hotel parking lot, I grabbed a sandwich from a beach-side stand. I walked along the beach and found myself thinking about the letter in the bottom of my desk drawer. What would Charles do if I chose to go? Would he really leave me like he had planned? I stopped when I reached the place where we were supposed to do the dolphin swimming. I spread out the towel that was in my beach bag and laid down to bask in the sun while I waited for 4 o'clock. The heat of it felt amazing on my skin. I was going to have a perfect tan when I got back home.

⟳

JULIUS GRABBED US EACH ANOTHER beer from the fridge. "So, do you want to watch the basketball game tonight?"

"Actually, I'm meeting Kalea for dinner. I should really head out soon." She just got back from her honeymoon last night. We had planned to go to dinner so we could catch up. Nothing had happened to me since her wedding. All I had done was wallow in heartache and loneliness. But I was sure she'd have a bunch to tell me.

"Don't you think that's going to be a little awkward given your recent epiphany?" Julius asked. He turned on the television—the basketball game was about to start.

"Yes, but I can't say no. No matter how I feel, I'm still her best friend and I would rather be her best friend than be nothing to her." I put my unopened beer back in the fridge and put my shoes on.

"Well, tell her I said 'hi' then. I hope she had a terrific time on her honeymoon."

"I'll try to remember that."

I walked to Gigi's, the small Italian restaurant that Kalea had chosen for dinner. Why did I agree? It was a small, romantic restaurant with dim lighting and slow, love music playing in the background. I was about to pull out my phone and cancel when I saw her.

She was wearing black, dress pants and a beautiful red cowl-neck blouse. Her hair was done up in curls that bounced as she tapped her foot to music only she could hear. Her skin was a deep golden colour, as if she'd been tanning her entire vacation.

"Well, you can't say it was raining on your honeymoon," I said.

She threw her arms around me. "There you are. I'm not used to your lateness anymore. I was beginning to think you were going to stand me up."

"I'd never stand you up," I said and led to her to the door. The waiter sat us at a small table next to the window. We quickly decided what we wanted. She always got spaghetti and meatballs at Italian restaurants. I settled on the linguine. We didn't speak much as we enjoyed our food and each other's company.

"It was beautiful in the Bahamas. I wish you could have come along. Charles was sick most of the trip, and so he stayed in the hotel room. I mostly hung out on the beach and swam. I also took this tour through an underground aquarium. I saw all sorts of fish—manta rays, angel fish, puffer fish, clown fish, parrot fish. It was astounding."

"That sucks that he was sick most of the trip. Did he do anything with you?"

"Well, we went for dinner once to this little restaurant. But no, we didn't get to do anything else. He was too sick."

"Did you get to swim with the dolphins like you wanted to?"

"Yes, I did. It was magic. Best thing I ever did in my life."

We strolled out of the restaurant.

"Are you walking home? I asked. "Or do you have the car?"

"I'm going to walk home. Do you want to join me?"

"Sure, I'm staying at Julius' tonight. It's not that far from your place."

I LOVED SEEING ALEXI AGAIN. Throughout dinner I could barely pay attention to our conversation because of how gorgeous he looked. His brown eyes sparkled in the dim lights, and his curly hair looked so soft. I wanted to wrap my fingers in it. Why did I have to choose such a romantic restaurant for dinner?

I was really starting to think I had made a mistake marrying Charles. Charles was sick our entire honeymoon. And it was as if he hadn't even cared. I kept telling myself that I was just having cold feet; but seeing Alexi again made me think otherwise. It made me realize how much I liked Alexi.

I had been so worried about what I wore tonight. Not that I would ever cheat on my husband, but I wanted to look attractive so I that could tell if Alexi wanted me as much as I wanted him. However, his actions and expressions didn't give me any hint that he was interested in me. It slightly saddened me, but when he agreed to walk me home, I was thrilled.

We walked to the park by my apartment, lay down in the grass and looked up at the stars. We had been doing this since we were about fourteen—laying in the grass for hours, counting the stars, and dreaming.

He glanced at me. "It's getting really late. Charles is probably going to want you home soon."

"Charles isn't even home tonight. He went over to Josh's place to watch the game and enjoy chicken wings. He planned on crashing there tonight."

"Not home, eh? So, you can do what you want tonight?"

"Yeah, I could."

"Are you happy, Kalea?"

"I don't know, Alexi. I thought I would be. And I should be." I thought about how different my life would be if I hadn't married Charles. I had changed my mind about going to school for him. He didn't want to be with someone on the other side of the world. He said he would leave me if I went away to school. I changed all my dreams to be with him and, lately, I had been wondering if it was worth it. "I just got married for crying out loud! I should be honeymooning and having the best days of my life. Instead, it feels like he doesn't even know I exist."

"I'm sorry, Kalea. I wish I could make it better for you."

"It's not your fault that I might have made the biggest mistake of my life. I just wish I could go back and say no. It hasn't even been a month yet, and I don't think I can take it."

"You'll get through it."

"I hope so."

And then he whispered: "I love you, Kalea. I always have."

"Goodness, I've missed you. I love you, too. Geez, what's gotten into you? Why are you all serious suddenly?" I said playfully.

"I mean it. I love you. I'm in love with you. And I need you. I want you to be happy, and I don't want another day to go by that I don't have you in my life. I need you." And then he kissed me with all the passion in the world

"Alexi, we shouldn't…" I started, but a wave of desire washed over me so fierce that it left me breathless. He pulled away, but I pressed my lips back against his and kissed him deeper.

Chapter Four

Kalea's kiss ignited a pulsing fire inside my entire being. I couldn't think straight. A part of me wanted to push her away, but when she opened my pants and reached down to cup me, I was lost to her. There wasn't anything I wouldn't give to her, even if it meant hell later.

I trembled as her fingers touched my shaft then slowly moved down to its base. My breathing turn ragged as she softly cupped me. I felt like I was going to burst as she skimmed the underside of my manhood, which made me all the hotter for her.

I peeled her clothes off slowly. I wanted to feel her skin against my own. I trailed my hands over her body, savouring every bit of it, every dip and curve.

Pulling back from her, I tore my clothes off and pulled her hard against me. The feel of her soft skin against my own left me dizzy. I ached to be inside her body. I would give anything to be married to her. I wouldn't spend our honeymoon trapped in the hotel room by myself. Sick or not sick, I would make her beg me for mercy from my questing hands and lips.

Kalea arched her back as I gently teased her nipple with my tongue and fingers. Slowly, I touched the part of her that I craved the most. I lost control, and I buried myself inside her wetness. I heard her moan, and I took her hands in my own while thrusting against her warm body.

I slid my hand down to tease her cleft as I was already on the verge of release. I didn't want to slight her. I wanted to make her feel the way a married woman should feel. Her orgasm started the moment I kissed her, while my fingers still played with her.

***

ALEXI FELT AMAZING AS HE slid his hard body deep inside my own. I arched my back as far as I could to feel the full depth of him. It didn't take long before something inside me burst apart, and I felt my entire body shudder around his.

Alexi moved ever faster. My pleasure left me dizzy. Each of his deep, passionate thrusts took me higher than the last. I cried out as I felt him release inside me. He gasped and collapsed slightly. With his warm body against mine, I didn't want to move.

Regrettably, he pulled back, careful not to leave my body as he kissed me. I could see the passion and love behind his eyes before his eyes suddenly cleared. A look of horror appeared on his face. He pulled himself away from me and reached for his clothes.

"What's wrong?" I asked, freezing cold with his departure. "Alexi, what's wrong?"

"You're married, Kalea. What have we done?" He put his face in his hands and looked like he was about to hurl. He yanked his clothes on.

"Alexi, it's not that simple …"

"No, Kalea. It is that simple. I can't believe you would even let me do that. You know how I can't stand people who do this. You're married. You're supposed to be sleeping with your husband, not everyone else."

"Alexi, I'm sorry. I wasn't thinking, Alexi, please stay. We need to talk about this," I said without even thinking to be offended by his comment.

"Kalea, I can't. I can't stay. I can't even look at you right now," he cried as he rushed off.

"Alexi, please! Don't go!" I shouted after him. Tears ran down my face. He didn't look back as he stormed off in the direction of Julius' house.

I felt empty and cold from what we'd done. But I also realized that I needed to leave Charles. He wasn't the man I was in love with. Alexi was. How could I not have seen it before? Then again, if I were being honest, it was just that I had never acknowledged it before. I felt sick to my stomach as I pulled my clothes back on and walked towards my house. Even with my arms wrapped around myself, I couldn't get any warmer. I knew why though: Alexi's anger had caused a coldness to seep inside my heart. It wouldn't leave easily.

I STORMED INTO JULIUS' APARTMENT. He looked up from the television. "Okay, you look angry as ever. What the hell happened?" Julius asked. I didn't want to talk about it, but I knew that he wouldn't let up, especially with me being as angry as I was.

"I had sex with Kalea," I said simply. I went to his fridge, downed a beer and grabbed two more. I handed one to him then sat down beside him on the couch.

Julius gasped, then paused the recorded television show. "You what? You do realize that she's married, right?"

"Yeah, I know. That's exactly why I'm pissed. How could she do something like that?"

"Um, I hate to break it to you, buddy, but I'm pretty sure that it takes two to have sex … at least any sex that I've ever had."

I gave him a droll look as I finished my beer and grabbed another one. "She knows how I feel about cheaters. She could have stopped me."

"Uh huh, I'm so sure that's the case. You're in love with her … passionately. I don't think anything including a hurricane or tornado could have stopped you from having her. You need to stop blaming just her, and realize that you're also to blame."

"Shut up, Julius."

"I'm serious. I think you're angrier with yourself than her. You ignored your morals to be with her. It was only a couple of years ago that Drea cheated on you. You probably still remember how it felt. You did claim to be in love with her after all."

"Drea has nothing to do with this. I hate her guts. I'm not mad at myself. I'm not the one who cheated on my husband."

"Drea has everything to do with this. And again, I'm sure you were a willing participant in tonight's events. If Drea hadn't hurt you as badly as she had, I'm sure you would feel differently about what you did. I'm sure you'd still feel bad, but I don't think it would be quite this extreme. So, what happened after, anyways?"

"I stormed off. I told her that I couldn't even look at her right now, and I left."

"Wait a minute. Are you saying that you left her, naked, wet and cold? You told her, the woman you're in love with, that you couldn't stand to look at her?"

"That about sums it up."

"You're an idiot. I think you just ruined your life. She'll never forgive you for that one." He turned off the television and headed to his room. I heard him rustle around in his room for a little while before he climbed into bed.

It was stupid and inconsiderate of me to treat her the way I did. Julius was right. I was an idiot. She had to forgive me. I may never forgive myself for causing her to cheat, but I needed her to forgive me. I couldn't live with myself otherwise.

Chapter Five

I spent the night in the living room crying my eyes out. I had no idea what to do. I loved Charles; at least I thought I did. But I had never felt passion for him like I had felt for Alexi last night. If I let it slip through my fingers, I was certain I would never find it again.

Alexi had always been my best friend. We were closer than ever. I couldn't stand to lose him, but I think that by sleeping with him, I was going to. Drea had cheated on him, and he had never gotten over it. He had always been against cheating, but Drea had made him even more certain how wrong it was.

He couldn't stand anyone who hurt someone else for a night of sex. He hated anyone who would be so selfish. The thought of Alexi hating me broke my heart in two. It brought tears to my eyes. However, the thought of hurting Charles because of cheating on him didn't faze me in the least. And the thought of Alexi hating me for loving him? That broke my soul to pieces.

I had to break up with Charles. I needed a divorce. I couldn't do this. I couldn't live without Alexi. Somehow, I was going to make this right. I didn't know how to ask Charles for a divorce, so I would have to think more about that. But some way, somehow, I would be with Alexi.

I couldn't sleep at all after I got home from the park. I had called Candace to try to talk to her, but her phone had been off. I left a short voicemail telling her that I had slept with Alexi and then I hung up. I needed to talk to her. I couldn't stop thinking about how Alexi would never forgive me.

Charles didn't get home from Josh's house until almost noon. I didn't want to talk to him. I was afraid that I would accidently slip and tell him what had happened. He had been jealous of Alexi when we had first started dating.

He had thought that Alexi and I were more than just friends. But over the years that we had been together, he had gotten over his jealousy. Who would have known that all those years ago, Charles would have been right?

He wasn't home for long though. He was home to eat lunch and then he had to go into the office to sort out some business matters for his trip the following day. They had to go to California to speak with some corporate lawyers to put the finishing touches on some of the policies for the company.

He planned to be gone for three entire days. Given the thoughts that were circling around in my head, I was perfectly okay with him being gone. I needed to figure out a way to get out of my marriage with Charles. I also needed to figure out a way to get Alexi to forgive me.

—◦

I WOKE UP TO SOMETHING smelling like bacon. Julius always had bacon for breakfast, no matter what else he had. Today it was bacon and pancakes.

"Feeling any better since you had a chance to sleep on what you did last night?" he asked and put a plateful in front of me.

"No, I still feel like shit. But I'm mad at myself for not being able to control myself with her. You would have thought that my moral character and conscience would have stopped me from kissing her in the first place."

"Wait a second. You're telling me that you kissed her first and then proceeded to treat her the way you did last night? My goodness, you're a bigger idiot than I thought."

"I know. You don't have to keep reminding me. I'll guess I'll just have to wait and see if she'll ever speak with me again," I said and listlessly poked at my breakfast.

"She's not going to forgive you. You treated her like she was someone to be used then disregarded. Woman don't usually take well to being used."

"That's not what I did, and you know it."

"You and I may know it, but I'm pretty sure that she doesn't know that. You still haven't told her how you feel about her."

"That's not true, I did. I told her right before I kissed her. I told her that I loved her and that I needed her."

"Well, at least you did something right. Then again, though, women always think that men will say anything to get in their pants."

"So basically, I'm screwed."

"Yep, I'd say so."

"What am I going to do? I need her, Julius. I'm in love with her. I always thought that I was in love with Drea, but this feeling, it blows that one out of the water."

"You can't do anything."

"I have to."

"Well, you can't. There's nothing you can do until she leaves her husband. It's not like you can ask her to leave him. That'd be mean, considering you were her man of honour. If you were going to ask her to leave him, you should have spoken up before the ceremony."

"Maybe I'll get lucky and she'll have enjoyed that as much as I did. It might even make her leave him."

He laughed. "I can guarantee that she didn't enjoy it as much as you. You broke her heart to pieces, trampled on her feelings and then bolted."

"It's not funny, Julius. I didn't mean to hurt her. I hope she can forgive me for what I've done."

"I think you need to forgive yourself as well. She's never going to see a reason to forgive you, if you don't see a reason to forgive yourself first."

"How in the world am I going to forgive myself? I was mean and inconsiderate to her after our little, well, body connection."

"Is that what you're calling it now?" He chuckled and then started to get ready to go to work.

I opened the door. "I should be heading out. I'll swing by later to watch the game if you want," I said.

"Yeah, sure." He called from the other room.

It wasn't long before I was sitting on the couch in my own living room. I had stopped by the beer store on my way home from Julius' place and picked up two cases of beer. I put in a movie to watch, but I wasn't paying any attention to it.

I couldn't stop thinking about Kalea. It wasn't fair. I had my chance to tell her that I had loved her for fifteen years now. Why would I wait until now to realize how I felt? Now, after she had married someone else. I was an idiot, that's for sure.

I kept replaying last night in my head. It was the best sex I had ever had. I had been with other girls before, and they had felt good, but nothing could compare to how I felt while I was making love to Kalea.

Why couldn't I tell her how I felt? So, what if it ruined her marriage? Charles was an asshole. Clearly, she wasn't happy with him, or she never would have allowed to me to touch her, let alone have sex with her.

But I knew I couldn't do that. I couldn't push her to leave Charles. She might end up hating me for making her leave him. But if she concluded that she needed to leave him, I would be completely fine with that. Then maybe I would get a second chance.

My doorbell rang, scattering my thoughts. I glanced down at the various empty bottles of beer on my coffee table before heading towards the door. I had just reached it when it swung open and my mom entered.

"Why in the world did it take you so long to answer the door?" she said. "I know you're not at work today. Theo called and said you were sick. You don't look sick to me." She bustled inside and placed a quart of soup on my kitchen counter. She also had a bag of goodies from the drugstore.

"I'm not sick. I just needed a day off, so I figured I would use one of my sick days."

"Well, why would you need a day off? It's not like you have girlfriend issues or anything." She looked around my living room. "Don't you know how to clean up after yourself? I could have sworn I raised you better. Empty beer bottles everywhere. What is the matter with you?"

"Mom, I'm fine. Can you just leave me in peace today? I don't really want to talk about it."

"Fine, this time you get a free pass, but only because I'm late for lunch with your father. We don't get to go on dates as often anymore because we're just too busy for them. Tonight, he may get lucky, though, as long as he forgives my lateness."

"Mom, I didn't need to know that."

"Well, how in the world do you think you were created?"

"I don't. I don't think about that ever. EVER," I said and walked her to the door.

"Ugh, fine. I love you. I'll be by in a couple of days."

"I love you, too. Goodbye Mom."

When she left, I sat back down on my couch and opened a fresh beer. My stomach started growling though, so I ended up ordering a pizza. I wanted to call Kalea, but I didn't think that enough time had passed. And I knew that I should apologize for what I said to her, but I just wasn't ready yet.

Thankfully, the doorbell rang with my pizza. I paid the guy and sat back down in the living room. I paid attention to the romantic comedy I had put on as I sat and ate. I wanted to see Kalea again, but I knew I couldn't. There was no use dwelling over what I wanted to do and what I should do.

Chapter Six

❧

Charles had left on his business trip with Josh that morning. He had told me that he wouldn't be back for three days. That gave me three days to figure out what I was going to do. If I stayed with Charles, I would never be able to look at Alexi. Our friendship would be over. Fifteen years of friendship over because of a marriage that I wasn't even happy in.

Or I could leave Charles—break his heart because of my selfishness and go off to be with Alexi. We could be happy together, and I could return to school to finish my degree. He would never stop me from what I wanted. But we could only be happy together if he forgave me for cheating on Charles.

If he couldn't, then I would be alone. I could still return to school, but our friendship would still be over. What had I done? For a single night of passion, I may have ruined the friendship with my best friend forever. That thought made me sick to my stomach.

I put a horror movie into the player and lay down onto the couch. I had already brought down my blanket and pillow. I pulled them closer to me and tried to focus my thoughts on the movie instead of the huge problem that kept floating around my thoughts.

Slowly, I drifted off to sleep…

I woke up in a large bed with the sun shining in the sky. The drapes were blowing in the open window and the clock said 9:45 am. I slowly rose from the bed and went out into the hall. The house was unfamiliar. I made my way down the stairs and into the kitchen.

There was a framed wedding picture of Charles and me in the hallway. There was note on the fridge that read: "Don't forget to take your meds today. They're on the bathroom sink. ~ C."

I went into the bathroom that was near the kitchen and, sure enough, there was a bottle of anti-depressants on the sink prescribed to myself. I went back to the kitchen and opened the fridge. My stomach was growling in need of food and I figured there would be something that I could find in there.

The fridge was full of takeout containers, empty or half full of food. There were no fresh vegetables and not a single piece of fruit. I guess I wasn't eating anything out of there.

Suddenly, the doorbell rang. It was Julius.

"What are you doing here?" I asked and pulled my robe around my shoulders.

"I came to make sure you were okay after last night." He said as he came inside the house.

"What do you mean by that?" I asked. I couldn't remember anything from the previous night. It was as if it didn't exist at all.

"You called Alexi's cellphone, screaming that he was going to kill you. Your voice was shaking and terrified. It's all in a voicemail on Alexi's phone. Alexi can't stand to talk to you so he ignored it. I listened to it today and thought that I would come and make sure you were okay. Did you take your meds today?"

"I saw them, but I haven't taken them yet. What do you think could have happened last night?" I asked and followed him into the kitchen.

He sat at the kitchen table. "I don't know, but I'm assuming it has something to do with the bruises on your face, neck and legs today."

"Bruises on my face?" I asked before I rushed to the bathroom. I looked in the mirror. Sure enough, the entire left side of my face was blackened, and it looked like handprints on my neck. I slowly removed my robe to reveal even more bruises covering my skin. There were welts across my back as well, as if I had been hit by something that looked like a metal rod.

"You should probably take your meds while you're in there. I don't want another call from the hospital saying that you tried to kill yourself again." I heard from the other room. Tears welled up in my eyes.

I came out of the bathroom "I tried to kill myself?"

"Okay, now you're starting to scare me. Maybe we should take you to the doctor to make sure you didn't get a major head injury."

"No, it's okay. I'm fine; you should get back to whatever you were doing. I'll be okay." As I said those words, I had a sinking feeling that I wouldn't be.

After Julius left, I spent most of my day watching movies. At around 6 o'clock, Charles came home. He was angry from his day at the office. Without even a hello or a kiss, he went straight to what appeared to be a liquor cabinet and pulled out a bottle of whiskey. He took a long drink before he poured himself a glass with ice in it.

He sat down at the kitchen table and finally looked at me. "Where's my dinner, woman?" he snarled. He looked me up and down. "You know I don't like to punish you the way I do, but if you would ever do anything right for once in your life, I wouldn't have to." He downed his glass and stood up.

"I didn't realize you wanted dinner," I said. I opened the fridge to see what I could give him for dinner. It was too late, though, I felt his fist connect with my shoulder. I fell to the floor. He grabbed the tire iron from the cupboard beside the sink and started beating me with it.

As the blackness started to overtake me, I knew I needed to get out of there. I couldn't live this way any longer.

I awoke startled from the terrifying dream and saw the movie credits rolling on the television. I had the sinking feeling that the dream I had was a premonition, not just a nightmare. I couldn't let myself be the victim of that. I had to do everything I could to prevent that from happening.

I got up, switched the movie to a romance movie and returned to the couch. I had to think of a way to break the news to Charles without him becoming the monster in my dream. It didn't take long before my eyes fluttered shut once again.

This time I woke up in a small apartment. The sound of a child's laughter drew me to the living room. There, in the middle of the living room floor, was Alexi and a little girl. She looked up and shrieked the moment she saw me.

"Mommy! Mommy! Come play with us!" She called. She ran over and took me by the hand and led me to the floor.

"Good morning, beautiful," Alexi said as he pulled me into his arms and kissed me.

"Yuck, Daddy." The three of us laughed.

"Would you like breakfast? Ally and I made waffles. We made you some."

"I would love to have some. Thank you both," I said and kissed Ally on the head. How amazing that this beautiful little girl was my daughter. I walked to the kitchen and poured syrup over my plate of waffles with blueberries.

"Time to go to school Ally, grab your backpack and I'll take you to the bus stop." Alexi said as he rose from the floor and went to the door and put on his shoes.

"I love you, Mommy. Have a good day," Ally said. She gave me a hug and a kiss before she grabbed her lunchbox from the fridge and put it in her backpack. Alexi came over and kissed me goodbye before they left.

It didn't take long before Alexi was back. I was already done my waffles, and I had gone to get dressed. I had the weirdest feeling that I had to get dressed to be somewhere. He came up behind me and wrapped his strong arms around me.

He handed me my bag and car keys. "Have a good day at work. You better hurry up, though; you're going to be late. Your students will think that they don't need to be at school today."

As I walked through the door to the hallway outside, I heard a phone ringing in the distance...

I woke up to my cell phone buzzing on the coffee table in front of me. It was Candace. I had left a voicemail to tell her that I had slept with Alexi, but we hadn't spoken about it yet. I was sure I would get an earful as soon as I answered.

Chapter Seven

"What took you so long to answer? This is the third time that I've called."

"I'm sorry, I was sleeping. It takes a while for me to answer, you know."

"Why in the world would you be sleeping in the middle of the afternoon?"

"I don't know I guess I fell asleep watching this movie."

"Well, whatever, so I got a message that you slept with Alexi. Details please."

"What do you mean details? I'm married, I never should have done it."

"Sure, but you couldn't help yourself. He is pretty gorgeous after all. His tanned muscles and his lovely dark locks.

His penetrating stare and his goofy grin, the one he always wears when you're around. He is actually quite dreamy …"

"Would you stop it? I don't need any reminders on how gorgeous he is."

"Then tell me how it was."

"It was fine. Well, more than fine. I'm in love with him, Candace, and I have no clue what to do about it. I need him."

"Wow, now that's a pretty loaded statement."

"I'm not joking, Candace. What am I going to do?"

"Well, first of all, you need to decide who you want to be with: Charles or Alexi. Then you need to decide how you're going to be with that person. If you choose Charles, then you probably shouldn't be friends with Alexi anymore because that could be tempting and your cheating might happen again. If you choose Alexi, then you need to figure out how you're going to break it off with Charles. It's quite simple really."

"Candace, I have no idea who to choose. I kind of think I love them both."

"Well, then, let's weigh the pros and cons of each one. We shall start with Charles because it would be easier to just stop being friends then it would be to finish things with Charles…"

"Yeah, right, I could never stop being friends with Alexi. Other than you, he's my best friend."

"Whatever … What do you like about Charles?"

"He treats me nicely. But he's always working and he's never around anymore. He discourages me from certain things like going to school. He wants me to stay home. He wants a wife, not a partner. I hate his friends. They always make me feel inadequate."

"Okay, fine. In summary, he sucks and the only thing good about him is that he doesn't hit you."

"That's not exactly what I said."

"Whatever, onto Alexi."

"Well, I don't know. He's my best friend. He would never discourage me from going to school. He would treat me as his equal."

"Well, according to what you've said in this conversation, I think you should go with Alexi. However, I also think that you should go with him because your eyes sparkle when you're near him. He always makes you laugh and smile. Charles is never around and he always sides with his friends."

"I still don't know."

"Well, I would love to talk more on this, but I really need to go. You should talk to Alexi. If you truly love him, you owe it to both of you to give it a chance. Anyways, I should get to class. Love you, bye."

"Love you too."

Well, that didn't help me any. She didn't help tell me how to break up with Charles. I guess I still needed to figure that part out on my own. Maybe I needed to think it over for a few days though. Maybe Charles could change my mind when he got back.

Maybe I wasn't in love with Alexi. Maybe it was just the adrenaline from the other night that kept me thinking that I didn't want to be with Charles anymore. Maybe I just needed to remember why I married Charles to begin with.

I decided that I was going to wait until Charles came back. I would spend time with him as his wife. After a few weeks, if I still wanted to be with Alexi, I could leave Charles then.

Chapter Eight

I decided to go to a bar because I ran out of beer. I hadn't stopped drinking since I had gotten home from Julius'. Most of the time they had a beer delivery service and I didn't need to leave my house to get more. However, they had closed earlier and I needed more.

I figured I would go out, have a few drinks and hopefully catch some live music. I was always in the mood for some good tunes. I wanted to come up with a way to get Charles out of the picture. I knew he didn't treat Kalea the way she was supposed to be treated, but I didn't know how to get her to realize that also.

I remembered when we were in high school and she had first started dating Charles. I kept trying to tell her that he was an asshole and wasn't any good for her. She didn't believe me. It was the first and only time that we quit being friends. She said that she couldn't be friends with someone who couldn't respect her own choices.

It was the hardest six months of my life, and I seriously thought it would never end. It ended because of an argument that her and Charles had. She came running for comfort and because I was lost to her, I gave it to her. She accepted that I couldn't stand Charles. I became blissfully ignorant of how he treated her, and we hadn't fought over that since.

I wanted to talk to her. I needed to get her to see who he was. It was then that I saw him. He was supposed to be on a business trip until Thursday. He shouldn't even be in the same city. Thankfully, I was sitting in the back of the bar at a booth.

He strode in as if he were the king of the world and walked right up to a lanky blonde standing by the bar. He leaned over and kissed her as she handed him a beer. Who in the world was that? She didn't have any right kissing Charles.

I knew I was being a hypocrite, but I couldn't take it. I downed the last of my beer and sauntered up to him.

"Now, what in the world are you doing with this woman? You're married, aren't you?" I said. He turned to look at me.

"It's not what you think, Alexi." I couldn't stand to listen to him so I punched him square in the jaw. The blonde shrieked as he stumbled backwards.

"I don't want to hear it, Charles. You married Kalea. You're the luckiest man in the world to have her, and you're just going to throw it away for some random woman?"

"I'm not some random woman. I've been with Charles for four years now. You have no right to be treating him like this." She said and crossed her arms.

"Alexi, listen, it's not like that. Just forget you ever saw me here."

"Not like what Charles? Not like you're cheating on my best friend and expecting me to forget about it?"

"I'm not cheating on her. She knows about Hannah."

I didn't want to hear his voice any longer, so I struck him again and again until the bouncers of the bar pinned me against a wall. They called the police. The only injury noticeable on Charles were the bruises on his face. He didn't look any worse for wear anywhere else on his body.

The police arrived and handcuffed my hands behind my back. They told me that I would have to spend the night in the drunk tank to wait and see if Charles was going to press charges or not.

I really hoped that he had the courage to charge me. Kalea would want to know exactly what happened between us for him to press charges against me. I kind of thought that once she found out that I attacked him because he had been cheating on her for four years, they would break up.

He already didn't treat her right. He stopped her from doing the things that she loved best.

They put me in a small cell by myself. There was only a small cot and a toilet, and the only thing I could see outside my cell was the hallway that led back to the main part of the police station.

There was a guard in the hallway, but I couldn't have cared less about that. It's not like I wanted to go anywhere anyways. I really wanted Charles to press charges because then Kalea might see how much he sucked. Then I would get my second chance.

I lay down on the small cot and thought about how my life would be with Kalea. We would move into a big house. She would go back to school. She had always wanted to study literature. Our big house would have a library in it. I could already see her sitting on the porch in a swing reading the latest romance novel or murder mystery.

Maybe she would even get a job as a librarian or a teacher one day. I think she would love that. I also saw a baby in our future together. At first, I imagined a baby boy but that didn't seem right. I wanted a little girl—beautiful and strong—just like her mom. I fell asleep with the thought of Kalea rocking our daughter to sleep.

I was rudely awakened by someone banging on the cage-like door to my prison cell. I looked up to see Charles snarling at me. Was he here to press charges against me? I hoped so. I smiled up at him with a hopeful glint in my eye.

"We need to talk. Preferably without your fist connecting with my face."

"Ahh, but that was so much fun last night. I can still see a slight bruise where I punched you that first time."

"I'm not pressing charges against you. The last thing I want is for Kalea to know about Hannah. I can't live without Hannah in my life."

"Then why in the world would you marry Kalea?"

"Because that's what was expected. My parents don't even know Hannah. If I suddenly told them that I was marrying her, they would have freaked. I care about Kalea. I don't want to hurt her."

"Then, why are you? Just break up with her. Let her find her happiness."

"Yeah, it's not that simple. I knew you wouldn't understand. There'll be two thousand dollars transferred into your bank account this afternoon. Kalea is not to find out about Hannah. Have I made myself clear?"

"Crystal clear, but I'm not taking your money. Know why? Because I can't promise that I won't tell Kalea. I'm her man of honour. It's my job to protect her happiness and you? You're clearly a hazard to it."

"You tell Kalea and I will seriously fuck up your life."

"Yeah, and if I ever see you with Hannah again, I will dance in your entrails."

Charles glared at me then he stalked off.

I sat back down on my cot, just then the guard came and unlocked my door. He led me through the police station and out into the parking lot. Then the guard went back to work. I wanted to tell Kalea so badly. I wanted to run to her and scream that she had made the worst mistake of her life. But I figured she would chalk that up to me wanting to be with her. And that she would be right about.

In my opinion, love sucked. Especially when the person you were in love with was married to someone else.

❧

I WAS WAITING IN THE living room when Charles got home on Thursday evening. I was expecting him to come in and see me. Instead, he went straight upstairs and into his office.

I shook my head, thinking about how he didn't seem to want to see me even though he had been gone for three days; I went upstairs and stood in the doorway of his office. He was sitting at his desk with his head in his hands waiting for his computer to turn on.

"Aren't you even going to say hi to me?" I asked. I leaned against the doorframe and crossed my arms.

He glanced up at me, then logged into his computer. "Hi."

He seemed more interested in spending time with his computer than with his own wife.

"I have something I need to talk to you about," I said before I could stop myself. I had planned on giving it at least a week, but it seemed as if I wasn't important in the least bit to him. I guess it was time to leave him.

"I'm a bit busy now. Maybe later we can talk."

"It's important. I'd like to talk about it now."

"Look. I've had a long few days and right now, you're the last person I want to see. I can't deal with your whining."

"Whining? What are you talking about? You've been gone for three days and I'm your wife. You're supposed to want to spend time with me."

"Well, at the present moment, I've got work to do."

"Fine, then I want a divorce! This is not how a marriage is supposed to be."

"And where exactly are you going to go? You don't have a job or even a hobby for that matter. No one is going to rent an apartment or even a room to someone without a job. I guess that means that you can't have a divorce."

"Well, anything would be better than this marriage. I want to go back to school, Charles."

"They won't let you back into school. Now why don't you just forget this whole divorce thing and go to bed or go watch a movie. I need to get to work and you're not helping my mood at all."

"Do you even care about me anymore?"

"Of course, I care about you, you're my wife." He finally rose from his chair and pulled me into his arms. "I have missed you, but I do, really, have a lot of work to do."

I pushed him away. "No. I want a divorce. I need one. I'm not happy here. I don't think I'll ever be happy here with you. I need to follow my heart, and it's telling me that I made a mistake marrying you."

"I do care about you, but right now the marketing business is taking off and I need to focus on that. I may never get a chance at this again. You just have to be patient. Things will get better eventually."

"That's just it, Charles, it'll be years before the business is finally at the point where things can change."

"Kalea, please, give me a break, I'm doing my best."

"Charles, I did give you a break. I'm not happy, and I'm leaving. I'm going to stay at Julius' for at least a week. I'll arrange to have my stuff picked up when I get a chance."

I didn't give him a chance to respond. I grabbed my suitcase from our bedroom and rushed downstairs. I put on my shoes and coat, only then did I look up the staircase. It didn't surprise me in the least that he hadn't followed me. I waited for a moment before I left, thinking that maybe he would change his mind. When he didn't come after me, I shook my head and left.

~

I FIGURED GOING OUT TO a bar again was a bad idea, and so instead I simply went to the beer store and bought ten cases of beer. I didn't want to run out again. I called the delivery service as soon as I got home and ordered two more cases of beer. I figured I could keep my stock up so I didn't go out to a bar and run the risk of being thrown in jail again.

It's not like I didn't already know that drinking was bad for me, but I needed some way to forget about my bleeding heart. I had originally thought about heading over to Julius' to clear my head, but for some reason I just wanted to stay at home.

I had just sat down with a beer to watch episodes of a reality crime show when my cell phone rang. I checked the call display before answering.

"Yes, Theo?" I half-chuckled into the receiver. Theo was my boss. I should have gone to work both yesterday and today, but I really didn't feel like laying drywall.

"Where are you? You were supposed to be at work yesterday. Are you all right?" he asked.

"I'm fine. I just don't feel like myself."

"Well, you need to be at work tomorrow or else I'm going to have to start looking for your replacement."

"Whatever, Theo. I'll see you tomorrow then," I said and hung up the phone. I couldn't stand him. He was always just sitting around and not doing any work. I understand that a site supervisor has paperwork and things to do, but he should be helping his workers also. We never had enough guys on the job site; it would help immensely if he would contribute.

After the call, I put my show back on and went back to my beer. I was still angry with myself. After everything Drea put me through, I still slept with Kalea. I thought my control was stronger than that, but when it came to Kalea, I lost all of it. I'll never forget the day that I found out about Drea's cheating.

It was in this very apartment. I came home from work early because it had started to rain. I heard laughing coming from the bedroom. For a moment, I simply thought that it was her watching a comedy on my bedroom television, but then I heard a guy's laughter also.

I flew into my bedroom, work boots tromping dirt. There she was in all her naked glory with both of her hands tied to my bedposts. There were two guys in the room. One was Brian, a guy from work who usually installed windows. The other was a guy I had never met. Both were naked, just like Drea.

She tried to explain that they were raping her, that they had tied her down and were taking turns having her. I didn't believe it for a second. She had been laughing when I came into the apartment, after all. Not long after that I had found out about just how many guys Drea had slept with while we were supposed to be engaged.

The pain of that day shot through me as I remembered how much I had felt for Drea. Those feelings were hogwash compared to feelings I had for Kalea. I remembered the vow I gave myself that night as razor blades sliced my soul to shreds:

I swear I will never cause someone else to cheat on their husband, boyfriend or fiancé. I will not be the reason that someone else's heart is shattered.

There were only two people who knew about my vow: Julius and Kalea. It was ironic that Kalea would be the one I broke it for.

⸻

TWENTY MINUTES AFTER I LEFT my house, I showed up at Julius' soaking wet from the rain. Luckily the rain disguised my tears, but I had a feeling that Julius knew I'd been crying. I put my suitcase in the living room and tried to dry myself off as best as I could.

He took my suitcase and headed down the hall. "I cleaned up the spare room. Alexi usually just stays on the couch, but since you'll be here for a bit longer than a night, you get special privileges."

"Speaking of Alexi, he doesn't know I'm here, right?" I called after him. I removed my shoes and sat on the couch. I had known Julius almost as long as I had known Alexi. Julius and Alexi had been friends since they were eight, so it was just expected that I would get to know Julius as well.

"I didn't tell him," he said. "He's still pretty mad at himself over what happened between you two." He pulled out two root beers and brought them to the living room.

"He told you?"

"He tells me everything. But you're welcome to stay here as long as you need. However, if you don't want Alexi to know, you probably shouldn't stay too long."

"I don't know. Candace thinks that I should head back to school. Maybe go to New Zealand to spend time with her, study literature like we planned."

"Yeah, Alexi isn't going to like that, but I know it would be good for you."

"I don't know. I'm so confused right now. I have no idea what I want. A fresh start sounds like the best thing but fresh starts are always the hardest. I think the dreams I had really tuned me into what was happening with Charles. I never want him to treat me the way he did in that dream."

"What dream? How did he treat you?"

"Oh, I forgot, I haven't told anyone about them. Umm, well, the other day, I had two dreams about how my life could be, I guess. Anyways, in the first one, it was like a premonition on how my life would be if I stayed with Charles. I was kept at home all the time and if something wasn't perfect when Charles came home from work, I'd get punished for it. It seemed like he was an alcoholic, an abusive alcoholic.

You were in the dream. You came over because you were worried about me. You're the one who told me about all the bruises on my skin. You also told me that I had tried to kill myself. I was on anti-depressants, and I clearly wasn't happy with my life. You had only come over because Alexi hadn't forgiven me about what had happened. I still don't think he's ever going to." I sipped my root beer. Julius had listened carefully the whole time, a quizzical look on his face.

"Wow, that's extreme. Do you really think that he'd become like that? Or do you think that the dream is making what's really going on seem worse?"

"I don't really know, maybe. I really liked the other dream, though. It was the life I would lead with Alexi. We had a beautiful daughter, and I had a job that I loved. It was perfect, just like, well, like a dream."

"Ah, I see. So, in the dreams, Charles was a horrible husband, someone who never made you happy and beat you to a bloody mess. Whereas Alexi treated you with kindness and gave you a life you'd always dreamed of. I kind of understand your confusion now."

"It's not that simple, though."

"Well, it never is. But Charles isn't completely horrible. You did marry him after all. He had to have made you happy at some point."

"I guess so. But he couldn't even be bothered to say hello to me when he got home from a business trip. It's as if he didn't miss being with me at all. I want someone who's going to miss me when I'm gone."

"I think everybody wants that. Well, it's getting late. There's a bunch of movies underneath the television if you want. I have to work in the morning so I'm headed off to bed. If you're hungry the fridge is fully stocked, but if you want something specific just write it down and I can pick it up tomorrow. Goodnight, Kalea, sleep well."

"Goodnight, Julius."

"Oh, and Alexi will forgive you, but he needs to forgive himself first. Just give him some time."

I didn't stay up and watch a movie. Instead I went to the spare room, stretched out on the bed and stared up at the ceiling. I thought about the two dreams that I had had and how opposite they were. Maybe Julius was right. Maybe the dreams were making reality seem worse than it really was. Either way though, there was only one thing I was sure of: I didn't want to be with Charles.

Chapter Nine

As soon as my plane touched down in the Christchurch International Airport in New Zealand, I saw Candace's golden curls bouncing as she ran and threw her arms around my neck.

"I've missed you so much. I know we talk all the time, but it is so much better to see you in person. So, I moved into a bigger apartment to make room for you. There's no point in you staying in residence if I already have an apartment rented. I'm so excited, you're going to love it here."

"I've missed you, too." I laughed as we grabbed my suitcase from the belt and headed off. It didn't take us long to get to the new apartment Candace had rented, even with the streets packed with vehicles.

It was just down the street from the university so that way we wouldn't have to spend money on buses or cabs to get to class, we could simply walk. The apartment that Candace rented wasn't even as big as Julius' back home. It had two small bedrooms, a bathroom and a kitchen with a tiny living room attached. The living room was only large enough for the couch, coffee table and television stand that Candace had already set up.

The bedrooms were so small that Candace had put our dressers in each of the closets so we could put small computer desks beside our beds. It was a good thing that I had only brought along a few books instead of the six bookshelves full that I had put in the storage unit with the rest of my things from Charles' house.

Julius was taking care of the rest of my things that wouldn't fit in the storage unit. He was going to tell Alexi that I had left; I hadn't been able to bring myself to tell him. I was still confused about my feelings for him. I was just going to focus on my literature studies and, if I still felt that I had feelings for Alexi when I got home, I would try to do something about them.

There was nothing I could do without Alexi's forgiveness anyways. He couldn't stay mad at me forever, could he? We'd been friends for countless years, which had to make up for my brief absence of moral character that one night. I wouldn't be able to live with myself if he didn't forgive me.

Candace came into my room and plopped on my bed. "How's it going in here? Is your tiny suitcase unpacked yet? I'm starving and there's this great place I want to take you to."

"I actually haven't started unpacking yet, but we can go grab something to eat. I wouldn't want you to starve to death," I teased. I grabbed my sweater and headed towards the door. She jumped off the bed and came with me. It wouldn't take me long to unpack everything. My thoughts were something else; Alexi's anger that night was forever branded in my mind.

IT HAD BEEN ALMOST A week since I had seen Julius. So, when I walked in the door to see boxes lined up in the hallway, I was completely baffled. Julius wouldn't move without telling me. He would have asked me for help, that's for sure.

"Julius? What are these boxes for?" I asked as I made my way to the living room couch. He was in the kitchen, making himself lunch.

"They belong to Kalea. She needs to keep them here until she comes back or until she finds a bigger storage unit. I just haven't had time to move them into the spare room yet.

"Back from where?"

"Uh, New Zealand. Yeah, I was supposed to tell you that she decided to go back to school, so she joined Candace in New Zealand to study literature. She didn't really have time to tell you herself before she took off. It was kind of a last-minute decision."

"She's gone? Wait, Charles let her go back to school?"

"Not exactly ..."

"What do you mean, not exactly? Charles knows, doesn't he?"

"Yeah, I think he knows, but I don't think she cares what he thinks anymore. Considering they're not together anymore and all."

"What do you mean, she left him?"

"Yeah, actually, she was all confused about who she was in love with, so she left him, and decided that, until she figured it out for herself, she'd go to New Zealand with Candace and study her literature."

"So, it's my fault? I broke her marriage?"

"Well, actually, he came home from one of his business trips and he didn't even bother to say hi to her even though he had been gone for three days."

I couldn't believe what I was hearing. Kalea left Charles. She left him! He had never treated her right. In the beginning, Candace and I had tried to tell her that he wasn't right for her, but she refused to believe us. He was always more interested in his friends and his work than he ever was in her.

When they would fight, I'd go over to her place, watch movies with her while she cried for hours. He had never wanted her to be anything more than a plaything. At first, she fought it. She wanted to work, go to school, and have a life. Charles didn't want her to though. He had convinced her that long distance relationships didn't work and that if she went to New Zealand for school, he wouldn't wait for her. She thought she was madly in love with him; she felt she needed him and him leaving her was her worst nightmare. It was about time she realized she didn't need him to be happy.

I was consumed by the happiness I felt for her. She was finally going to be able to make her dreams come true instead of waiting for Charles' dreams to come true. It hurt slightly though, to know she didn't tell me herself. I got up from the couch and made my way over to the fridge where I grabbed two beers for Julius and me.

"It's not even one o'clock, I don't want a beer yet."

"Suit yourself," I said. "I'll drink for both of us." I'd been drinking quite a bit since I had seen Kalea last. I had wanted to apologize to her countless times, but I hadn't been able to bring myself to it.

"What's gotten into you? You used to barely drink at all," Julius asked as he watched me down the first one and then open the second.

"I don't know. It hurts. I just wish things were back the way they were. I miss her and I've tried to get myself to go and talk to her, but it doesn't work. It's like there's a wall now where their never used to be."

"What in the world are you talking about? You hurt? You have no right to hurt. You treated her like crap because you both couldn't keep your pants on."

"I know I did, and I can't stand myself for hurting her. I've played that night over and over in my head from the moment I agreed to walk her home. She was so beautiful with her dark curls rolling over her shoulders and her eyes! They sparkled that night. I haven't seen her that happy in a long time.

But every time I try to call her, or go see her to apologize for reacting afterwards the way I did, I can't do it. The second I do apologize, I feel like it will be the last time I ever talk to her. I don't want it to end."

"It wouldn't be the end of your friendship; you guys have been friends for fifteen years. That kind of thing doesn't just disappear. Besides, she's waiting for you to forgive her. She doesn't think you're going to," he said and took his plate back out to the kitchen.

"There's nothing to forgive her for," I said, puzzled.

He sighed. "The last time you guys saw each other, you both slept with one another. Then you told her that you couldn't stand to look at her anymore, that you were ashamed of what she had done. Then you left and stormed over here. In her eyes, she's done something wrong to make you as angry as you are. Therefore, you need to forgive her. Are you with me yet?"

"You don't need to talk to me like I'm stupid. I tried to block out what I said to her. I shouldn't have said any of it. I shouldn't have freaked out the way I did. Charles was probably really pissed at her, wasn't he?"

"Honestly, I don't think he knows. Or cares for that matter. He didn't even come after her the night she left. He didn't call her. He didn't come over, even though he knew she was here."

"She came here the night she left him? She usually comes to my place for things like that."

"Yes, but remember that wall you told me about. The one that you feel is there now between you and her. She feels it too. She doesn't think she can talk to you about this because, well, the dream she had about you."

"She had a dream about me?"

"Uh, yeah, it was one of the things that prompted her to leave Charles. Actually, she had two dreams. One where Charles was an abusive alcoholic, and she was beaten every day. In that one you never forgave her. The second one was about the life she could have with you. A good job. A loving husband. And a beautiful daughter named Ally."

I couldn't think straight as an image of Kalea holding my daughter went through my mind again. She would make a wonderful mother. I missed her so much. I couldn't breathe for a moment as I sat there, shell-shocked by what Julius had told me.

"I should go. I have to meet my mom. She's worried about me."

He took my empty beer bottles and put them in the kitchen. "She should be, you're turning into an alcoholic."

I HADN'T EVEN BEEN IN New Zealand a week and I had been to eleven different restaurants. They were the best Candace had found. I missed Alexi profusely. I had tried calling him a couple of times, but I always hung up before it started ringing. It scared me to call him. I didn't think he had forgiven me yet. I could only hope he would be able to.

I was lying on my bed reading *Jane Eyre* by Charlotte Bronte when my dad called. He was worried about me because I hadn't called him in a while.

"Where have you been, Kiddo? I haven't seen you since your wedding," he asked

"Remember how I told you that I got accepted to the University of Canterbury?"

"Yes, I remember, you put the letter in your desk in case Charles changed his mind about long distance relationships."

"Well, I decided to go anyways. So, I'm in New Zealand studying literature like I wanted. I used money from the account to pay for it. I hope that's okay."

"Don't worry about the money. It's there for you to use for school. You didn't even bother to come and say goodbye though?"

"I'm sorry, Dad. It was a last-minute decision."

"And what exactly does Charles think of the matter? Did he go with you?"

"No, Dad, Charles and I separated. He was more interested in his marketing business than he was in me. I never really saw it for the longest time, but I don't think he really loved me."

"My goodness, how long has it been since we talked?"

"It's been a while, hasn't it?" I laughed.

"Girl, we got to go, it's time for class," Candace called from the other room.

"Sorry, Dad, I have to go to class, but I'll call you when I get a spare second. I love you."

"I love you, too, Princess. Be happy," he said as he hung up. I grabbed my pack and rushed out the door after Candace.

Chapter Ten

✤

After a short bus ride, I arrived at the small café down-town where I was meeting my mom. She was a scary woman at times. When anything bothered my sisters or me, she knew instantly, and she would do anything to make us happy again. But I was her baby, and she always protected me the most. I could tell by her expression as I walked in the door that she was ready to break someone in half.

I pulled up a chair next to her. "Hey, Mom, how are you today?"

"You're late as usual. I thought I raised you better than that." She scowled and waved the waitress over.

"You did, Mom, but I like to keep people on their toes." I laughed as I ordered myself a black coffee.

"So, are you going to tell me what's wrong with you lately?"

"I just miss Kalea. She went to New Zealand to study with Candace," I said vaguely.

"That's not what Julius says."

"Would you quit talking to my friends before you talk to me? It gets really annoying and it makes these visits seem irrelevant."

"If you would tell me the truth, I wouldn't need to talk to Julius or Kalea at all."

"You talked to Kalea?"

"No, not this time, but I have before."

"Yeah, well, she doesn't want to talk to me right now, so I doubt she'd talk to you."

"What did you do to that poor girl now?"

"Excuse me, I thought I was your child, not her."

"You are, but Kalea is like another daughter to me."

"You have Jenna and Sash for that."

"Would you just get over it already and tell me what happened?"

"I'm in love with her. I watched her marry someone else. I accidently hurt her more than I ever should have and I can't forgive myself no matter what I do."

"You mean because you slept with her and then told her that you couldn't stand to look at her anymore?"

"If you already know all that, then why in the world are you still asking me what happened?" I scowled.

"Because you're my son. I love you and I can't stand to see you hurting this much. You need to forgive yourself. It's not your fault that you're in love with each other but you're both too damn stubborn to admit it. You need to talk to her. With what I understand, she left Charles to be with you. You can't let your true love pass by without fighting for it."

"It's not that simple, Mom, and you know it."

"Well, you still need to talk to her. Let's go, I'll give you a ride home."

"Thanks Mom," I said. I got up from the table and followed her to the car. It wasn't that easy to get rid of her though. I love my mom and all, but she wanted to come in and I really didn't think she would like the way my apartment looked.

Sure enough, she freaked out when she saw the empty beer bottles and pizza boxes strewn all over the place. She scowled at me and started her usual speech about how she raised me better than this.

"Mom, I don't want a lecture. I know I should clean up. I've just been a mess that's all."

"I hate to see you like this."

"I know. I will clean it up, I promise. Dad is probably waiting for you though, you should head out."

"All right. I love you. Please feel better and talk to Kalea."

"I love you, too. Goodbye Mom."

As soon as she left, I plopped down on my couch and grabbed a beer out of the fridge. I knew I should call Kalea but I wasn't ready for that yet. I really hoped she was doing okay in New Zealand with school and everything. Instead of cleaning up the mess, I added to it all night by drinking more beer and ordering another pizza. I missed her so much, but I was still angry about what I did and I was still hurt that I had caused the wall to come between Kalea and me.

I LOVED MY CLASSES. SOME of them were difficult and I didn't want to fail at any of them. I had been out of school for a couple of years. It took a little bit for me to get used to school again. However, I knew that school was where I wanted to be.

"Were going to be late. If only I hadn't grabbed that drink before class," Candace said as we rushed to our classroom.

Luckily the teacher was late also. We were going to Early literature. We had an essay due that day. I had done mine as a comparison essay about the differences between *The Iliad* and *Beowulf.* I was quite proud of myself for the way it was written. I hadn't been in school for a while so I didn't expect to get a high grade on it.

The only seats left were in the middle of the classroom. I had already learned that students tended to avoid that area because Mr. Frick always chose students from there to speak and answer his questions.

"Okay, class, let's get started. First, I need all of you hand in your essays. I know that electronic copies should be in the email box but the hard copies can make a pile here on the desk."

I handed in both mine and Candace's, then, with a sigh of relief, I returned to my seat. The class seemed to take forever as I thought about Alexi being halfway across the world. I couldn't stay focused. Thankfully, Mr. Frick hadn't asked for any opinions.

"Come back to planet Earth, Kalea," Candace basically shouted in my ear.

"I'm pretty sure I've never left the planet," I said. Realizing the class was over, I quickly packed up my bag and followed Candace.

"So, what's got you looking so mopey, anyways?" she asked.

"I'm not mopey."

"Yeah, you are. You're definitely moping around for some reason," she said and led me to her favourite place, the food court. She ate at least six meals a day. I was completely baffled by the fact that she wasn't six hundred pounds or more.

"Are you really hungry again?"

"Just because you eat like a bird, doesn't mean the rest of us have to."

"I don't eat like a bird."

"You eat two snacks and a single meal a day, and that's it. That's not even equivalent to a full day's worth of food. Besides you're changing the subject again. What were you thinking about in class?"

"Alexi."

"You haven't stopped thinking about him since you got here. You should call him."

"I want to, but I can't yet. I'm not ready for that."

"Well, you need to get ready for it. You need to discuss what went down between the two of you."

"Look, I've got homework to do and I really should get to it."

"What? You're just avoiding the topic, that's all. Have fun with your homework and your broken heart."

"My heart is not broken. I'll see you at home," I insisted as I left.

Soon, I was laying on my bed thinking about Alexi even more. I missed his jokes. I missed the way he was always late. I missed his quirks, and I missed his sexiness. I kept replaying that night in my head. Just thinking about it made me long to have him again.

I wanted to call him and tell him that I was in love with him still. But I couldn't. I couldn't be as vulnerable as I was that night. I wanted to tell him that I had left Charles to be with him. But I didn't want to lose him. I knew he was probably still mad at me because of what had happened.

Drea had been too much of a bitch towards him. He had vowed to himself that he would never cheat or cause anyone else to cheat. That night he broke that vow; he wasn't going to get over that for a long time.

—◦

I NEEDED TO CALL HER. I grabbed my phone and I dialled her number. I needed to figure out if she could forgive me or not. I knew I wouldn't be able to stop drinking unless I talked with her.

I let it ring twice before I hung up. I was too scared to let it go through. Sure enough though, my phone rang as the call display flashed a picture of Kalea. I should have known that she would call me right back.

It took every ounce of my strength to ignore Kalea's call. I missed her so much. I knew that I needed to speak with her, but I couldn't do it right then. I wasn't ready yet.

I felt like an idiot. I should have just answered her call. I grabbed a beer from the fridge and grabbed a piece of leftover pizza. I sat down in the living room where I turned on a cop reality show again.

I contemplated trying to call her again. I knew that I was acting ridiculous. There was something wrong, though. That wall was getting higher and higher. Now I didn't even want to attempt the crossing

It was then that my phone rang. It was my mother. I knew I had to answer this call.

"Hey, Mom."

"Hey, Darling. I need to make sure that you are coming to your sister's birthday dinner?"

"Yeah, I'll be there. I wouldn't miss it for the world."

"You better be there. The entire family is going to be there including Grandma. You haven't seen her in ages."

"I'm glad she'll be there then. I should go Mom, I'm eating lunch." It wasn't a complete lie, but I really didn't want to talk on the phone with my mom any longer.

"All right, then. I'll check in on you in a few days. Love you."

"Love you, too, Mom. I'll talk to you later," I said as I hung up. I immediately dialled Kalea's number. For the second time I hung up after a couple of rings. I was still too scared to talk to her.

What if she never forgave me? What if she did forgive me, but she didn't want to be with me? What if we ended up together but lost our friendship in the process? There was too much risk in talking with Kalea. I wasn't ready yet.

⁓

I THOUGHT NEW ZEALAND WOULD be the answer that I was looking for. I spent most of my days in classes, most of my nights studying. I was surrounded by people at school, and Candace was always around. But I was lonelier than I had ever been before. It had been two months since I had left Canada to come down here to study.

A fresh start had been what I had hoped for. But I couldn't forget about Alexi. I missed him so much that my heart felt like it was shattering every time I thought about him. I couldn't stand to be away from him. I figured calling him might be the answer so I grabbed my cellphone from my desk and lay down on the bed.

I dialled his number and waited.

"Hello?" His strong voice answered from across the world.

"Hi, Alexi. It's Kalea. How are you?"

"Kalea? I thought you were in New Zealand."

"I am, but I've missed you," I said. Nothing but silence greeted me. "Alexi? Are you there?"

"I've got to go Kalea, I'm at work," he said and then he hung up.

Something felt wrong. He was never like that to me. Maybe he still hadn't forgiven me for what happened. He still couldn't be angry that I had cheated on Charles, could he? It had sounded as if he were hurting though. Now what did I do? I thought that he would be happy that I had gone back to school. I should have told him that I was going myself instead of having Julius do it when I was already gone.

I couldn't leave things the way they were between us. So, I dialled my Dad next. I needed to make arrangements for a place to live once I got back.

"Princess?"

"Hey, Dad. How are you?"

"I'm tired but good. How's school going? Did you get that essay back that you did on those books?"

"Yeah, actually I did. It had a few grammar mistakes so my mark isn't the highest, but I still got an 84%. I called because I was hoping you wouldn't mind me moving back home with you."

"You're coming home? Aren't you in the middle of a semester there?"

"I can't be here, Dad. It's too far away. I want to come home. I can try to see if I can transfer my program to a University there. But I would need a place to live."

"Well, your room is exactly the way you left it. You can just stay here until you find your own place. Or until you and Alexi straighten things out and you can move in with him."

"That's not funny, Dad. I don't think Alexi and I will ever be together that way, but I do need to fix our friendship. I miss him. However, I need to pack my suitcase and grab an airplane ticket. I love you and I'll see you as soon as I get home."

"I love you too, Princess. Have a safe flight," he said and then hung up.

In all of twenty minutes, I had my stuff packed and an airline ticket purchased. I had two hours before my plane left. Candace came in the door just as I hauled my suitcase out of my bedroom.

"Where are you going?"

"Home. I miss it there."

"It's about time you figured out that you belong there instead of here. I'm going miss you. Well, not the moping around and endless tears, but I am going to miss you. Tell Julius that I say hi and that he should call me."

"I do not mope and endlessly cry."

"Yeah, you do. You miss Alexi and your heart is broken without him. It's not home you miss, it's him."

"Whatever, I have to go, is this your way of saying goodbye?"

She pulled me into a huge hug. "I love you, Girly. I hope you have a safe flight. Please call me when you get to Alexi's."

"I love you, too, but I'm not staying at Alexi's, I'm staying at my Dad's." At that, I grabbed my suitcase and headed downstairs to get a taxi. A wave of relief washed over me when the plane took off from the airport. I was finally heading home and I finally knew where I wanted to be. It wasn't going to be easy, but I knew I had to fight for what I wanted.

Chapter Eleven

The whole time I was at work, I thought about what Kalea had said when she called. *I've missed you.* Since she left, I'd been waiting for her to call and tell me that. I had to call her back. I was going to do it as soon as I hung up, but my boss was nearby and I didn't want him to catch me goofing around on the job.

We were doing the framework on a house for a couple who were expecting a new baby. I also didn't want to be talking on the phone while hammering away at the nails and wood. I'd done that before and almost lost half my fingers in the process.

So, I waited the five hours before I tried to call her back. It went directly to her voicemail. She must be in class. I would have to try again later. I went straight home when I was done. I wanted to clean up the apartment some. My mom had planned on coming over again tonight to check on me, and I wanted it to look like I had my life back together.

I was still drinking heavily. I doubted I'd be able to stop unless Kalea either came home or I left for New Zealand. I didn't think she wanted me to go after her though. I think that's why she asked Julius to tell me instead of telling me herself. I don't think she felt what I did. She couldn't. If she did, she would have come to me before she even left.

The thought of her not loving me the way I loved her sent spears through my heart. My chest throbbed with the pain of it. I stopped cleaning up and grabbed a beer from the fridge. The only thing in my fridge was beer but, then again, with how I felt lately I was okay with that.

I was into my sixth beer when mom showed up. She wasn't the least bit impressed with the state of me or my apartment. I had thrown in a movie to wait for her. She didn't even stay long enough to talk. She took one look at me, shook her head in disappointment and left.

I thought it might be a good idea to call Kalea again. Hopefully, she would answer this time. However, I just reached her voicemail again. Why did she have her phone off? Or had she just blocked me? It had been ten hours since I had spoken with her. I should have just talked to her then. But as usual, I didn't do what I should have.

I kept drinking until I passed out on the couch. I wanted to feel numb but my entire body hurt too much. The alcohol didn't even help anymore.

——◦

IT FELT LIKE FOREVER BEFORE I finally reached home. I was completely exhausted by the time I got to my Dad's house. I had trouble sleeping on the airplane, and the flight was twenty-seven hours in total, and that didn't include the hour and a half car ride to get to my Dad's house.

I went straight upstairs and into my old bedroom. Dad wasn't home when I arrived. I assumed he was at work. I pulled back the covers of my bed and crawled inside. It wasn't long before I was asleep.

"So, Princess, what time did you get in? Dinner will be ready shortly if you're hungry," Dad said as he sat on the edge of my bed. I glanced groggily at the clock where the time said 7:15 pm. I had slept for a good eight hours.

I guess around eleven. I was so tired though, I just slept the rest of the day away." I gave him a big hug. "Wait, why is dinner so late?"

"I usually have dinner at 6:30, but I thought I'd let you sleep. You seemed like you needed it. You don't want to sleep too long though, cause then you may not sleep tonight." He went to leave the room. "I'll be in the kitchen waiting for you. Oh, and I'm starving, so please be quick."

"Okay, Dad. I won't be long I promise." I climbed out of bed and into my bathroom. When Mom died, Dad gave me the master bedroom; that way I had my own bathroom attached. He said that I would need it more than he would. It had only been six years since she died, but it still hurt to think about her. I missed her a lot.

I quickly drew a brush through my hair and washed my face. Then I headed downstairs to have dinner with Dad. I went into the kitchen to the smell of Mom's cabbage rolls cooking.

"Since when did you learn how to cook?" I asked as I savoured the smell of the cabbage and the tomato sauce.

"I found your mom's recipe books, the ones that she put together. They're really easy to follow and I guess anyone can cook really." He sat down at the table and I joined him.

It tasted the way I remembered it did. Dad had been able to follow Mom's recipes. It tasted amazing. I helped him clear the table when we were finished eating. We were about to start the dishes when my phone rang. It was Alexi.

I WAS TERRIFIED TO TRY to reach her again. At some point, there had to be a time when her phone wasn't off and I feared what she'd say. I couldn't bear the thought of her dismissing my feelings.

My mom had told me that I needed to talk to Kalea, but she didn't exactly say what I was supposed to say to her. Various scenarios played out in my mind. I wanted to tell her that I was happy that she was in school again. I wanted to tell her that I understood why she didn't tell me. I could understand if I wasn't what she was looking for, but I couldn't stand the distance that had grown between my best friend and me.

I needed her back in my life. So, I took a deep breath, picked up the phone and dialled her number.

She answered on the second ring. "Hello?"

"Hi, it's me, Alexi," I stammered, terrified about what I had to say and then thought that it would be better to say what I needed to in person.

"How are you?"

"I'm tired. I was hoping that I could get your address in New Zealand; I was hoping you'd let me visit. I really need to talk to you."

"Oh, I'm not in New Zealand."

"What do you mean, you're not in New Zealand? What happened to school?"

"I'm trying to transfer to a different university. I didn't like it there. I missed home."

"So where are you now? Can I still get your address? I need to see you."

"I'm here, at home. Since you need to talk to me so bad, why don't we meet up at Blanca's? You know, the small coffee shop near the high school?"

"Sure, we can meet there. When though?"

"Well, I'll be there in twenty minutes. I guess I'll see you when you get there."

"That's it? Wait, when you said home, you meant here?"

"Goodbye, Alexi. I'll see you in twenty minutes." The phone clicked off as she hung up. I was going to see her. She was back in town. I looked down at myself. I was a mess. My hair was all greasy. I was only wearing my boxers, and my skin was sticky from spilled beer. I needed to shower and shave before I could even think about seeing her.

It took me twenty minutes to simply get showered and shaved. It would take me at least another fifteen to get to the coffee shop. I thought of calling her, but she knew I would be late anyways. As I was rushing out the door, I ran into something solid. I looked up. It was someone, not a something.

Charles. He looked pissed off. Behind him Josh, Gregory, Matthew and Stewart glared their mutual hatred at me.

"Well, boys, it looks like we won't have to go find him. Seems he's just going to run to us," Josh piped up.

"Look, I have to meet someone, I don't have time for your bullshit today, Charles," I said as I tried to get past them.

"A little bird told me about what you and Kalea did the day after we got home from our honeymoon. They said they saw you two together … 'cuddling' in the park," Charles snarled and crossed his arms.

"Look, Charles, if you'd have treated her right in the first place, maybe she wouldn't have been up for 'cuddling' with me in the park," I said and tried to get past once again. Josh and Stewart blocked my way.

"So, it's true then? You were together that night. My little bird wasn't just imagining it?"

"Charles, I don't have time for this, I have to go."

"I want her back. I need her back. I love her; she's my wife. She belongs at my side. I gave her everything. She didn't have to work. She didn't have to go to school. And she could spend her time on her hobbies, like reading."

"That's not the life she wanted and you know it. Besides, you had someone on the side anyways. Why don't you just have her? Hannah, was it? She didn't like your cheating ways, either?" I saw the rage billowing in him, just below the surface of his eyes. He was going to explode. I should have stopped there, but I wasn't thinking straight. "You weren't good enough for Kalea. The life you gave her was making her unhappy and you knew that."

At that, he punched me in the face. I tried to fight back but Matthew and Stewart pinned my arms behind me. He kept hitting me until I saw stars and his boys threw me on the ground.

"I am good enough for her. I'll have her back, hypocrite. You can guarantee that. Once she sees how worthless you are, she'll come crawling back. Let me guess, you didn't even tell her about Hannah yet? So, you lied to her. She won't ever forgive you for that either." He left, Josh, Stewart, Matthew and Gregory trailing behind him.

I could feel the bruises forming on my face. The blood poured out of my nose; I could taste it in my mouth. I spit as much of it as I could out on the sidewalk as they went off into the distance. Kalea wouldn't take him back, not after the dream she had about him.

He was right, though, I hadn't told Kalea about Hannah yet. I hadn't even had the courage to tell her that I missed her. I didn't want to tell her. I wanted to protect her. I knew that it was pointless to tell her when she had left him anyways. It would only hurt her to know what she had been blind to for four years.

I looked at my watch. They had made me thirty minutes later than I had been originally. I would be lucky if Kalea was still there when I showed up at Blanca's. Everybody stared at me as I walked into the café.

I was about the leave when I saw her sitting by the window in the back. She had on a plain green shirt with half sleeves and a black skirt with blue and green flowers on it. She was gazing out the window, sipping her tea. She looked lost in space. She was beautiful. My nerves crept up on me as I walked towards her.

"Do you need help?" The waitress behind the counter asked, concerned.

"No, I'm okay," I said as I kept walking.

She reached out with a stack of napkins. "But you're bleeding. Don't you want a napkin at least?"

"Oh, sure," I said as I remembered that I was bleeding.

Kalea looked up when she heard me talking to the waitress. She must not have seen the blood. She simply smiled as I made my way over to where she was.

"You're bleeding! What happened? Are you okay?" she asked as I sat down and wiped the blood from my face.

"I'm fine, but I think we should get out of here. Everyone is staring at me as if I'm about to start a fight."

"Well, that's probably because you look like you were just in a bar brawl."

I led her out of the café. "Yeah, well, I'm not the one who started it. Did you tell Charles that we uh … well, slept together?"

"You called me all urgent to talk to me about Charles?"

"No, no, but it's why my face was bashed in," I said as we headed in the direction of Julius' house. He lived the closest and I needed a washroom to wash my face.

She stopped on the sidewalk. "Charles did this? Why in the world would Charles come after you?"

"He claims that he heard from a little bird that we cuddled in the park the day after you came home from your honeymoon. So, Charles and some guys came after me while I was on my way over here."

"You have got to be kidding me. I swear to god, I'm going to have some words with him. He has no right to come after you the way he did."

"I don't think it's me that he's going to go after. He wants you. He says that he'll have you again."

"Okay, that's kind of scary," she said as we knocked on the door of Julius' house. Julius answered the door in only his pyjama bottoms.

He threw his arms around Kalea. "Wow, I thought you were in New Zealand."

"Actually, I came back. I got back this morning. Um, Alexi needs to borrow your washroom," she said as he led us into the living room.

"What the hell happened to you? Did you put your face in a meat grinder?" He asked as I went to the washroom to clean up.

"No, I didn't. I thought it would be fun to get beat up by Charles and his posse."

"Charles did that to you?" He asked and sat on the couch.

"Apparently, a little bird told Charles that Alexi and I … ahh… well, you know." She blushed and sat down next to him.

"Oh, so it seems he didn't take that very well," Julius mocked.

"I think my face is proof of that," I said as I joined them in the living room.

"My goodness. Maybe he does care about her," Julius laughed as he went and grabbed some beers from the fridge. Remembering that Kalea didn't drink beer, he also grabbed a root beer. The three of us spent the night goofing around and watching movies. Kalea slept in Julius' guest room and I spent the night on the couch. It wasn't until after Kalea left in the morning that I realized that I still hadn't told her how I felt about her.

Chapter Twelve

"You were out late Princess. I hope everything is okay," Dad said as I came into the kitchen. I was hungry so I figured I'd grab something quick for breakfast before I confronted Charles.

"I spent the night at Julius' house because Charles beat up Alexi and we needed to get his blood cleaned up. Julius' was closer so we went there to clean him up."

"Charles did what?" Dad asked as he piled my plate high with pancakes and sausages.

"He punched Alexi a few times because he heard somewhere that Alexi and I cuddled … naked… in the park," I said, trying not to be weirded out that I was telling my dad that I slept with someone.

"You slept with Alexi? When? Kalea, were you still with Charles?"

"Yes Dad, I was still with Charles and, yes, I know it was wrong. I couldn't help it. You wouldn't understand."

"You're right I wouldn't understand. I raised you better. If you pledge yourself or vow yourself to another person, that vow is the most sacred thing in the world. You can't just break it like that, Kalea. Is that why you and Charles split? Charles found out about you sleeping with Alexi?"

"Dad, I know it's wrong. I never meant to hurt Charles. No, it's not the reason that Charles and I split up. Well, it kind of is, but not the way you're thinking about it. Sleeping with Alexi made me realize the extent of the feelings I have for him. It's one of the reasons that I chose to leave Charles. It's complicated, Dad."

"If you knew it was wrong, why did you do it?"

"Because I'm in love with him. I'm not in love with Charles. I want to be with Alexi so badly. I miss him. I need him," I said as I tried to eat my breakfast.

"Then why aren't you two together yet?"

"Because Alexi freaked out about what we did. Last night was the first time that I saw him since then. He said he needed to tell me something, but he didn't."

"Well, then maybe you should go see him again. This time, though, if you're going to spend the night away from home, please let me know so I don't spend *my* night worrying about you. I'll see you later. I have to get to the office." He kissed my cheek, and then headed out of the kitchen.

"Bye, Dad," I called. I picked at my pancakes. Thinking about everything with Alexi and Charles had made me lose my appetite. I scraped my plate into the garbage by the back door and put my plate in the sink. I went upstairs to wash up, and then I headed out to go meet Charles.

He would be at the office. I had twenty minutes before he went for lunch. I wanted to catch him on his break so I could yell at him in private. He had no right to attack Alexi. It had been my decision and my decision alone that had led me to leave Charles.

Hannah, Charles' secretary, led me into the conference room while I waited for Charles. She had said that he would be done in a few minutes.

"Kalea? I wasn't expecting to see you today. What are you doing here?"

"I need to talk to you. You had no right doing what you did to Alexi yesterday. What were you even thinking?"

He sat down in one of the chairs. "I was thinking that bastard slept with my wife and I don't like it."

"Look, Charles, yes, I slept with Alexi. Yes, I enjoyed it. I know it was wrong and I didn't mean to hurt you. Somehow, though, I don't think it hurt you all that much."

"You're my wife, of course it hurt that you slept with another man."

"We spent a week in the Bahamas and you spent the entire time nursing a cold instead of paying any attention to me. I may have been your wife, but I surely wasn't your love."

"Kalea, I was sick. You can't hold it against me for being sick on our honeymoon. I promised that I would make it up to you, but you never gave me a chance. I love you, Kalea. I want you."

"If you wanted me, you should have acted like it. You came home from a three-day business trip and didn't even bother to say hello to me."

"You're only saying all this because of what happened between you and Alexi."

"That's not true. I'm saying this because it's the truth. You kept me from doing the things that I wanted to do the most. I never should have agreed to be your wife. I should have left a long time ago. Leave me be, and if you ever mess with Alexi again, you'll be sorry." At that I left, and without looking back.

I wasn't thinking as I walked away from Charles' offices. I had nothing else planned for the day. Suddenly, though, I was starving. I stopped at a little bistro that was down the street from the offices. I grabbed a tuna-salad sandwich and hazelnut iced coffee to go.

I randomly walked in the direction of home. I was off in my own little world when I ended up in front of the house that Alexi and his company were working on. I could see Alexi inside, installing drywall. He wore jeans and a tank top while he worked away.

His muscles bulged as he worked. He looked like he should be on the cover of a magazine. His finely-tuned body sent waves of heat through me. He looked up suddenly as though he felt my eyes on him. His face lit up into one of his adorable half smiles.

I blushed as I waved slightly. He put down his tools and headed in my direction.

"What are you doing here?" he asked, standing close.

"I actually don't know. I went to speak with Charles. He shouldn't bother you again," I said. I noticed the bruises on his cheeks and eye. Even wounded he looked like he could take on the world and win. It didn't detract from his looks in the least.

"You didn't have to do that. I would much rather that he hurt me than you."

"Well, I better let you get back to work."

"Yeah, Theo will be really angry if he catches me not working. Why don't we grab dinner later?"

"Sure, where do you want to meet?"

"How about I pick you up from your Dad's at say six?"

"Sure, I'll see you then, Bye" I said, and watched as he went back to his work.

I then turned in the direction of my Dad's house. I had a dinner date with Alexi and I needed to figure out something to wear. I had to look my best. I couldn't stop thinking about what had happened the last time that Alexi and I had dinner together. I didn't think that I was ready for that to happen again yet.

I COULDN'T FOCUS AT ALL for the rest of my shift. I couldn't stop thinking about the way Kalea had looked with her hair in a messy bun, and her lithe body in that turquoise tank top, jeans and a green blazer that went so well with her turquoise sandals and white purse and brought out the green in her hazel eyes; it made them sparkle even more than usual. She always looked stunning, but green was truly her color.

"Alexi!" Theo's voice interrupted my thoughts.

"Yes, Theo?"

"We gotta get this drywall complete tonight. You can stay and help finish it off. You should be able to head home by eleven at the latest," he said.

"I can't stay tonight, I got plans," I said. My heart sank. I knew what his next words were going to be, and I didn't want to hear them.

"Well, then, maybe I need to hire someone else for the job. If you don't want to work, why would you want the job in the first place? What's more important to you, your job or your social life?"

"My job, sir," I said through clenched teeth. I wanted to tell him to shove it, but I knew that Kalea's birthday was coming up soon, and I wanted to get her something nice. That meant I needed this job.

"That's what I thought. I need this drywall up by the end of tonight. You can go home at eleven as long as it's all done," he said and then went back to do whatever it is he does. Nobody ever saw him working, but for some reason he was our supervisor.

I grabbed my phone and dialled Kalea's cell number. When I didn't get an answer, I tried her Dad's house.

"Hello?" Kalea answered.

"Hey, it's Alexi."

"Hi, I was actually just thinking about you."

"Oh, yeah, me too. Look, my boss is making me work till eleven. I'm not going to be able to pick you up. I was hoping we could go for dinner tomorrow instead."

"That's fine. I was going to call you and cancel anyways. My dad wants to do something with me tonight."

"Okay, cool, so I'll pick you at six tomorrow. I have to get back to work, though. See you tomorrow."

"Goodbye, Alexi."

I had the strangest feeling that Kalea had lied to me, but I didn't want to push it. I had a bunch of drywall to put up if I wanted to get out of here by eleven.

❧

I HAD NEVER ACTUALLY LIED to Alexi, but the thought of our date being cancelled hurt and I wanted him to think that I was fine with it. I missed him. I wanted to spend time with him.

My dad had called to tell me that he and his work buddies were going out after work today. He didn't want me waiting around for him. He knew that I would have cooked dinner and waited for him before I ate if he hadn't called.

Since Alexi had moved our date, though, I guess I was spending the night alone. Ever since mom died, I hadn't felt comfortable spending the night alone here in this house. I was fine when Dad was home, or when I was expecting him soon.

But Dad had said he would be late. Which meant I should probably call Candace. I could talk to her for a few hours and avoid thinking about the creepiness of this huge house.

I grabbed the phone and dialled her number. She must have been in class because her cell went straight to voicemail. I guess I would have to be okay in this big house by myself.

I could call Alexi to come over, but that would consist of me admitting to him that I had lied. That left me with two options: call Julius or go out somewhere alone. I didn't like the thought of going somewhere alone, and so I grabbed the phone and called Julius.

He answered on the third ring. "Hello?"

"Hey, what are you up to?"

"Not a lot. Who is this?"

"Oh, it's Kalea. Do you want to do something tonight?"

"Oh, hi. Sure. We could chill here or go out. Do you want me to pick you up?"

"Sure. How about twenty minutes?"

"Okay, see you then," he said and then hung up.

Fifteen minutes later, Julius rang my doorbell. I was ready, and glad to get going.

"So, what would you like to do?" he asked once we were buckled into his car and headed down the long, winding driveway.

"I don't know. I was supposed to have dinner with Alexi, but he had to work late."

"Oh, well, we could grab a pizza and watch a movie."

"That's sounds good. As long I don't have to be in my dad's big house."

"You never did like being there alone. Should we stop to pick up Alexi? I'm sure he's off my now. It's nearly nine o'clock."

"Actually, I kind of lied to him. I told him that my dad and I had plans when he called to cancel our dinner."

"What? Why in the world would you do that? If you would have told him the truth, he probably would have headed to your house the second he was off work tonight. You would be able to have some alone time together."

"Alone time would be awesome, but I don't even know if that's what he would want. It's nice being friends again though."

"Have you even talked about what happened?"

"About us? You mean about the night in the park?"

"Yeah, when the two of you … well, you know."

"We would have, but then Charles and his friends jumped Alexi and I was more concerned over that than anything else. I don't want to bring it up again because I don't want him to be mad at me again. I love him, Julius. I can't stand the thought of him being mad at me for loving him."

"He wasn't mad at you for loving him, he was mad at himself for not being able to control himself, even though he stood by at your wedding and let you marry that … that jackass. He was mad that he didn't admit his real feelings before that night."

"He has no right to be mad at himself for that. He's not the only one that hid his feelings. I did too."

Chapter Thirteen

It was nearly eleven thirty before I was finally able to leave work and head home. I crashed the moment I walked through my front door. I fell asleep on the couch, my work boots still on.

I woke up with sweat pooling in my socks and a painful cramp in my neck and shoulders. I undressed and took a shower. No chance to shave. I had to get to work again.

I had wanted to call Kalea before heading to work, but I didn't have time. I sure hoped she was still good to go out for dinner tonight. I pulled into work just as Theo was coming out the front door of the house that I had finished drywalling last night.

Theo opened the passenger door of my car and climbed in. "We need to get to the new house. The framing is all done, but we need to get the plumbing, electrical and drywall done," he said as he buckled himself in.

I put the car in gear. "Okay, where to boss?"

"682 Helena Creek Road," he said. He turned the radio from my favourite heavy metal station to one that played soft rock. Normally only I could touch my music, but since he was my boss and all, I let it slide.

We pulled up to the new house. It had only just been framed. Some guys were already working on brickwork and the roof. Thick grey clouds were forming in the sky. It wouldn't be long before the rain started.

Theo looked up, too. "Looks like we'll be headed home early today. We can't do electrical work in the rain."

"That's for sure." We headed inside where we found Paul and Zac. Brian had been fired for misconduct a few months ago. Paul was a plumber and Zac could do just about anything.

We only got two hours of work done before the clouds broke and the rain came pummelling down. A smile broke across my face. Theo told us we could go home and that he would see us tomorrow. I jumped in my car and headed to Kalea's house. It would be the very first time since I met her that I wouldn't be late. I was going to be early.

Helena Creek Road was right near where Kalea lived with her dad, and so it didn't take long before I was driving down her long, winding driveway. Her dad's truck was gone. He was probably already at work for the day.

I parked my car and walked up the stone path. I didn't bother ringing the doorbell. I had been accepted by both her parents and had my own key. Of course, I kept it in a box in my apartment and I never used it, but it was nice to know that they trusted me enough to give me my own key. I knocked gently before opening the unlocked door.

Kalea was in the kitchen having lunch when I walked in.

"Wow, you're kind of early," she said surprised. I sat down next to her.

I stole one of her cucumbers from her salad. "I know, eh? The temperature must have dropped in hell."

"Shouldn't you be at work?"

"It's raining. You can't do electrical work in the rain. I would get electrocuted."

"Oh, I see. Are you hungry? I could make you a sandwich and a salad if you want."

"Sandwich sounds great, but I can make it myself. You stay and enjoy your own lunch." I opened the fridge. I pulled out the brown bread, mustard, ham and lettuce and made myself a sandwich. I watched as Kalea nibbled on her salad. She never ate very much. I was surprised she was eating lunch at all.

"So, are we still on for dinner tonight?"

"Of course, why wouldn't we be still on?" I asked as I sat down next to her again.

"Because you're already here. You may not want to spend the entire day with me."

I sat in silence as I ate my sandwich. I wanted to tell her that I still felt the same way that I did that night in the park, but I couldn't bring myself to.

"You're my best friend. Of course, I want to spend time with you."

"Yeah, but you were mad at me, and we haven't been able to talk about that yet."

"Do you want to talk about it? Because I'm okay with just forgetting that it ever happened," I said as I finished off my sandwich.

"Forget what? Forget what we shared? Or just the argument afterwards?" she asked with a hurt expression on her beautiful face.

"I don't know …" I managed before a pounding at the front door interrupted me.

"Kalea, open up the door! I need to talk to you!" It was Charles and from the sounds of things, he was drunk and very angry.

"What in the world is he doing here?" she asked. She opened the front door. The second she did, Charles had his arms around her.

"I need you. I can't live my life without you. Whatever you need you can have it. I just need you," he slurred as he came further into the house.

"Charles, let go of me. It's over. You need to move on with your life," she said as she tried to get his arms off her. He wasn't listening to her. I felt my rage mount.

"Let go of her, Charles or you'll be leaving here in an ambulance," I said.

"What are you doing here? Are you with him? You goddamn whore. How could you? After everything we've been through together."

How dare he insult her! I lost control. I punched him in the face and felt his nose break beneath my fist. I hit him over and over until he cowered on the floor, covering his face with his arms. I looked up. Kalea was on the phone, calling the police.

"Alexi! What in the world were you thinking?"

"I'm thinking that he's a complete ass to you and that he just called you a whore and that he wouldn't get his hands off you when you told him to."

"That still doesn't give you a right to pummel him."

Just then the police and paramedics arrived. It was surprising they were so fast, but I guess for Charles that was a good thing.

"Believe me, that wasn't even close to what he deserves," I said as she scowled at me. The paramedics loaded Charles into the ambulance, they wanted to be sure he didn't have a concussion and he needed a few stitches and to have his nose straightened.

The police wanted to know exactly what happened to see if charges needed to be laid or not. Thankfully, they realized that Charles was drunk from his breath, and that he had been harassing Kalea, so they didn't stay long.

"I'll clean everything here up. It's my fault anyways." I said gesturing towards the blood on the floor.

"Okay, I'll go clear the table."

When I was done cleaning the floor by the front door, I went into the kitchen where Kalea was washing the dishes. I dried them and put them away. It was nice to simply be together. We still had a conversation to finish, but I figured that we could finish it later.

⁓

When we were done cleaning up the kitchen, Alexi stayed in the living room to watch a television show while I went to get changed for dinner. I was still upset that he wanted to completely forget everything that had happened between us. However, I knew I loved him.

I needed him to remember his feelings for me. I knew I would have to look my best. Then maybe he would realize that he didn't mean what he had said earlier. I didn't want to forget what happened between us. I needed him.

I chose a pair of black pin-striped dress pants and a bright-green flowy top that I knew brought out the green in my eyes. My mom had taught me what colours to wear to do specific things for my colouring. My shirt was bunched down both sides. It was off the one shoulder and that shoulder had a single spaghetti strap. I figured my hair would look best down, and so I curled it to flow in locks.

I pulled the necklace my mother wore to her engagement dinner out of my jewellery box, and clasped it around my neck. I took one last look in the mirror, and then I headed downstairs to where Alexi was waiting for me.

Alexi turned off the television and rose to meet me at the bottom of the stairs. "You look so beautiful."

"She does look beautiful, doesn't she? But, then again, she is my daughter. She gets her looks from me," my dad laughed while he came through the front door.

"Hey, Dad. We're just about to head out for dinner."

"Mr. Conwell. It's nice to see you again."

"Have a good time at dinner you two. See you tonight, Princess. And Alexi? Make sure she's home by eleven."

"I can do that," Alexi said and held the door open for me.

"So where would you like to go for dinner?" he asked the minute we sat down in his car.

"I don't know. You should pick this time I chose last time."

"You know that I can never figure out where I want to go to eat. It's simpler if you just pick."

"Fine, let's just go to the Rainbow Café. We love that place."

"Oh, come on, we always go there."

"Okay, fine. I've always wanted to try the food at Marino Palace. We could go there, but I hear it's pricey."

"There we go. Yes, we can go there. It doesn't matter how expensive it is. You're worth it."

I rolled my eyes and turned up the radio. He usually had on heavy metal music, so I was surprised to realize that he had a soft rock station on. It was love-song hour and they were playing love song after love song.

When we finally reached Marino Palace, I felt completely underdressed. I would have worn a dress had I known that this is where we were going. Everyone was dressed up. They had a valet service. We didn't even have to find a parking spot.

I'm surprised that they didn't have a dress code for a place as upscale as this. We were seated at a table near a window. The walls were decorated with expensive art pieces on a gold background. The chandeliers from the ceiling looked as if they were made of diamonds, and the carpet was a rich red.

Dinner was amazing. We decided to go play mini-golf before heading home. Alexi was always great at sports, and so it surprised me that I won our game. The drive home wasn't long enough. All too soon we were pulling into my driveway. Alexi told me to wait as he came over to my car door and opened it for me.

He walked me to my door, and then pulled me into a big hug. As I pulled away, I kept hoping he would kiss me. He didn't though. He just smiled and went back to the car. I waved as he pulled out of the driveway. I kept thinking to myself that I should have kissed him. I should have stood on my tiptoes and stolen a kiss from him.

I FELT STUPID AS I drove away from Kalea's house. I knew I should have kissed her. I knew I shouldn't have hit Charles. And I truly shouldn't have said that I wanted to forget everything that had happened between us. The truth was that I was terrified. I was terrified that she didn't feel the same way anymore.

I drove to Julius' apartment instead of heading home. I didn't want to look at all the empty beer bottles that were scattered throughout my apartment.

"Julius?" I called as I walked into his place.

"I'm in my room," I heard him call through his bedroom door.

I took off my shoes and walked through his living room to his bedroom. On his bed was a huge pile of books, and he was busy putting even more books on what looked like a new bookcase.

"What in the world are you doing?"

"My old bookcase broke. I bought this one today. It's supposed to have my books on it. That's what a bookcase does, holds books."

"I'm not stupid. I know that."

"Well, then why did you ask?"

"I didn't realize you had this many books. It's not like you read or anything. Now if this was Kalea putting ten million books on a bookshelf, I wouldn't even ask. But you? Where did you get all these, anyways?"

"I do read, thank you. I've had them forever. What are you doing here? Lately you've just been working and then going home and getting drunk, thinking about Kalea."

"I'm here because I didn't want to go home. I need to clean it up, and I'm procrastinating. I just had a date with Kalea. I took her to Marino Palace. I don't think it was technically a date, though."

"Marino Palace? That place is crazy expensive. It was a date, clearly."

"If it was a date, why didn't I have the nerve to kiss her goodnight?"

"Because, as I've said a million times, you're afraid of your feelings, and you're an idiot."

"I'm not an idiot. I'm going to watch a movie," I said, and I left him to his books and went to the living room. I opened his recorded movies and looked for the ones I'd never seen before and clicked on the first one I found.

Chapter Fourteen

I woke up the next morning; still thinking that I should have kissed Alexi. I got dressed, brushed my teeth, and headed to Alexi's apartment. I wanted to finish our talk from yesterday. I also wanted to kiss him.

I had it all planned in my head. I would stomp into his apartment, throw my arms around him and kiss him. Kiss him as passionately as I could. I wanted to tell him that I still needed him, and that I wanted to be with him. I wanted to tell him that I didn't want to forget about what had happened between us because I loved him. I loved him.

I opened his apartment door using the key he had given me when he first moved in. He wasn't home. It looked like an alcoholic's apartment. There were beer cans and beer bottles everywhere. It looked like the dishes hadn't been done in a week. His laundry basket was overflowing with dirty clothes. And his cat Moses was out of food. I wanted to sit and wait for him to come home, but I couldn't just sit in all the filth, and Moses wouldn't leave me alone. It seemed that he missed me more than Alexi did.

So, I threw a load of laundry into his washing machine and gathered up the beer cans and bottles. The junk filled four trash bags. Once the laundry was finished I started washing the dishes. I quickly switched the washing over to the dryer and threw in the second load before heading back to the dishes again.

I was interrupted by the ring of the doorbell. Alexi wasn't home, but I figured I should answer it anyways. It's not like someone couldn't tell that I was in here.

"What exactly are you doing here?" Alexi's Mom asked disgustedly as I opened the door.

"I'm cleaning. I showed up and Alexi wasn't here, but his place is a mess, so I figured I would clean it while I'm waiting for him to come home."

"Well, it's appropriate that you're cleaning it up, since you're the reason that it's such a mess."

"Excuse me? Linda? Did I do something wrong?"

"Yes, you did. You broke the heart of my son, and now you just think you're going to prance back into his life to stomp all over it again. I used to like you, but since you reduced my son to an alcoholic loner, I can't stand you."

"Linda …"

"I don't want to hear your excuses. I suggest you finish your cleaning and leave him be. He doesn't need someone like you to be his friend," she said, and then she turned on her heel and left.

I couldn't believe it. Linda used to treat me as one of her daughters. Her words echoed as I went back to cleaning the dishes. *You reduced my son to an alcoholic loner.* I did this to him? How in the world did I do this him?

It was his decision to become the way he did. But then I had slept with him and disappeared without him knowing that I had left. I couldn't stand the thought of me being the reason for Alexi turning into an alcoholic. I finished up the dishes, and wiped down the counters and tables. Then I finished the laundry, wrote a quick note to Alexi so he would know who had cleaned his apartment, and left.

I GOT HOME AFTER WORK to find that my apartment had been completely cleaned. My first thought was that my mom had come over and cleaned but, then again, she didn't have a key. Then I found Kalea's note. It was simple, really. It said that I should take out the beer containers, and that she had a great time at Marino Palace.

It made me happy to know that, like me, she had a great time on our date. I wanted to call her, but I saw my mom coming up the outside stairs. She would be pleased that my apartment was cleaner than the last time she was over.

I opened the door for her. "Hey, Mom."

"It's good to see that you're home this time. Is she still here?"

"She? Oh, Kalea? You came by while she was cleaning?" I said. I went into the kitchen and started to make myself dinner.

"Yes, her. You shouldn't be hanging out with her anymore." She sat on of one of the bar stools at the kitchen counter.

"Please don't start with me. I love her, Mom."

"You're too young to know what love is."

"Umm, you were my age when you married Dad."

"Whatever, I'm glad to see she cleaned up her mess. I'll pick you up on Saturday at around 4:30. We're going to dinner at The Dragon Restaurant for your sister's birthday."

"Yes, Mom. I'll be ready. Love you."

"Love you, too. Please stop hanging out with Kalea," she said one last time before she left.

I ate my dinner as I thought about what had happened with my mom. I knew she was angry at Kalea for hurting me, but I didn't think that warranted her asking me not to see Kalea again. She couldn't be serious. I had been friends with Kalea since I was twelve. I wasn't just going to throw that away because my mother didn't want me to see her.

I finished eating and quickly washed the dishes. I didn't want Kalea's hard work to be wasted. I was determined to keep my apartment clean. I was determined not to go back to drinking.

Before I forgot, I took the four garbage bags of beer containers down to the recycling room. I sorted out the plastics, metals and glass before I headed back to my apartment.

I filled up Moses' food and water dishes before I went to bed. It wasn't long before Moses joined me in bed. He curled up into a ball right under my chin and made it impossible for me to get to sleep. I gently moved him from on top of me to the pillow next to me.

I looked at the clock; it was 5:45 in the morning. I needed to get up at six to get to work. So, I hopped in the shower and started to get ready for work. When I got out of the shower, the phone rang.

"Hello?" I answered, leaving the bathroom.

"Hey, Alexi. We can't work today. It's raining like crazy outside. I guess I'll see you tomorrow."

"Oh, okay. Thanks."

"No problem," he said as he hung up.

I got dressed anyways. Kalea might be up for going for breakfast. Then we could probably finish that conversation that I had been avoiding. It was only 6:30 though. Kalea probably wasn't out of bed yet. I guess the worst thing that could happen would be for her not to answer the phone.

I dialled her number and after three rings I was surprised to hear her voice.

"Hello? Alexi? What in the world are you calling me this early for?"

"Hey, I just got a call from my boss saying that I don't need to work today. Since I'm already dressed and up and all, I was hoping maybe you would go for breakfast with me."

"Breakfast? Umm, I guess so. You would have to give me at least half an hour though, I'm not even out of bed yet."

"Yeah, sure, no problem. I'll pick you up at 7:15? Is that enough time?"

"Yeah, I'll see you at 7:15."

I grabbed my coat and headed out the door. I drove to the end of Kalea's drive way and parked my car. I sat back and enjoyed my music as I waited for it to be time to pick Kalea up.

I looked at the clock after a few songs. I silently cursed. It was almost 7:30. At least Kalea was used to my lateness. I always tried to be on time, but somehow the music often took hold of me, and I lost track of what time it was.

I drove the two minutes up her driveway and saw her sitting on her front steps. She yawned as I parked in front of her.

She climbed into the passenger seat. "You're late as usual."

"Technically I was here early. I was parked at the end of your driveway."

"Well, you should have just parked in front of the house, then I wouldn't have been waiting for twenty minutes," she joked as she turned the music down a bit.

"I figured we could go to Cora's for breakfast. Unless, of course, there's somewhere else you'd like to go."

"Cora's is fine. Wake me up when we get there," she said and leaned back and closed her eyes. She looked very peaceful as she pretended to sleep.

We were there in less than ten minutes. I looked over at Kalea. She didn't need me to wake her up. She was already undoing her seatbelt as I turned the car off. Although she looked half asleep, she was still gorgeous.

Chapter Fifteen

It's not like Alexi had never done anything like this before. He constantly called me up at all hours of the day to do something. I just wished it wasn't so early in the morning. I loved breakfast food more than any other type of food. The smell of waffles and maple syrup was the best thing in the morning.

We grabbed a table by the window, like we always did. He ordered French toast with apples and cinnamon, while I settled on blueberry waffles with sausages and fruit salad.

"So, do you want to finish our conversation from earlier?" Alexi asked as he sipped his coffee.

"What conversation?"

"Okay, then considering you can't even remember what we were talking about, I'll start. I never meant to say that I wanted to forget what happened between us. What I meant was that I wanted to forget my freak-out after what we did. I want to forget how I treated you afterwards."

"Alexi, we don't have to talk about this now."

"I still feel the same way I did that night, you know."

"What?"

"I still need you. I'm still in love with you."

Thankfully our breakfast came right then. I had no idea what to say to that. I wanted to tell him that I still felt the same way also, but I couldn't. I was still too terrified to admit it out loud. I had thought that I was ready to tell him how I felt. But I didn't think I was.

"I'm sorry. I didn't mean to freak you out. We can forget I even said anything," he said as he started in on his breakfast.

"We can talk more about it later if you want. I'm just really tired, that's all."

"Yeah, I guess I did wake you up too early, didn't I?"

"You did. So, let's just finish our breakfast so I can go home and go right back to bed."

"All right," he laughed as we continued our breakfast in silence.

After breakfast, Alexi dropped me off at home. I went right up to my bedroom and lay down on my bed. I stared up at the ceiling and thought about what had happened.

I felt like I an idiot. I choked when I should have told him how I felt. It must have been awful for him to express his feelings to me again and have me simply ignore him.

I should have told him that I loved him, too. But then where would we be? Linda hated me now because I hurt

Alexi. My dad wasn't too thrilled that I cheated on Charles. Everyone would judge us because of how we started dating. But then, why should I care, I loved him and he loved me?

So, I picked up my phone and dialled Alexi's cellphone.

"Hello?" Alexi answered almost immediately.

"Hey, where are you?"

"I'm just pulling into the driveway at my apartment. Why? What's up?"

"Nothing's up. I'm on my way over. Please don't leave," I said as I hung up. It was still raining outside when I got into a taxi. It only took twenty-five minutes to get to Alexi's house.

Well, this was it. I was going to tell him how I felt. Whatever happened next, happened. I just sure hoped he hadn't changed his mind since breakfast. I suspected that he was still feeling the same way, but that he would be hurt because of my delayed reaction. He might be afraid now because of my hesitation.

I raced up the stairs so fast that I nearly fell down them. Luckily, though, Alexi opened his door in time to stop me from falling back down the stairs.

"It's slippery outside. If you wanted to come over, I would have picked you up. You didn't need to take a taxi over."

"I love you, too."

"What?" he asked confused as I stood dripping just inside his doorway.

"You said earlier that you loved me. That you needed me. Well, I was shell-shocked. I love you, too, and I need you. It's why I came home from New Zealand. I couldn't live my life away from you. It's better to be friends then not have you in my life at all—" I was interrupted as his soft lips pressed against mine.

His kiss took my breath away. I pulled him closer. A wave of fierce desire pierced through me as his arms wrapped around me. His smile nearly reached his ears as he held me in his doorway. I shut the door so the rain would stop coming inside.

I smiled up at him. Finally, I felt like I was home again. I knew that I had been home for a few days, but being in Alexi's arms again made it all seem real. This was where I wanted to be, where I needed to be.

I DIDN'T WANT TO MOVE. I was quite content to hold Kalea by my front door for hours. My heart had grown wings when she told me that she loved me. I felt like I could soar through the sky like an eagle.

I knew I had to move though. I needed her even more than I had that night in the park. This time, I was going to savour her. I had to. She shrieked as I picked her up and carried her to my bedroom. The second I laid her down on my bed, though, Moses was on top of us.

"Go away, Moses. Can't you see I'm busy?" I grabbed him under his belly and locked him out of my room.

"Now. Where were we?" I felt her fingers moving gently through my hair as I returned to her and tasted every inch of her mouth and neck. I pulled her shirt over her head and off, and then I leaned in to kiss her more deeply.

I tried to control myself from moving too fast, but I could feel my control slipping. I wanted to make her feel amazing. She pulled my shirt off as she kissed me back. I wanted her so badly I didn't think I could wait another minute.

I slowly pulled her pants and panties down her legs and removed her shoes. I kissed my way from her toes to the triangle of brown curls at the junction of her legs. I felt her entire body tremble as I took the part of her I craved most in my mouth. I teased and tasted her until I felt her entire body release. With her sweetness on my lips, I kissed my way up to her breasts. I suckled and watched them pucker as I blew my breath across them.

When I couldn't control myself any longer, I removed my own pants and boxers. Her eyes were glassy as I finally pushed myself inside her. Her warmth surrounded me as I moved faster and faster. Her nails bit into my back as my hips thrust against her. When my release did come, I felt so dizzy from it, I almost passed out on top of her.

I never wanted to let her go again. I wanted her to stay here forever. She pulled the blankets over top of us and snuggled up under my chin. I held her close as we both drifted off into a blissful sleep.

Chapter Sixteen

I woke up with Kalea snuggled in my arms. I couldn't breathe as I felt the weight of my dreams finally within reach. I was never going to let her go again. I couldn't live my life without her. I slowly unwrapped my arms from around her trying to be careful not to wake her.

I went to the kitchen and started preparing Kalea's favourite breakfast—waffles. I cooked them to a crisp golden-brown and poured out some orange juice. I made sure to add fresh strawberries and blueberries to decorate the waffles, and then I heated the maple syrup. I was just finishing up setting the table when Kalea came out wearing one of my band t-shirts.

"Something smells absolutely amazing. You didn't have to make breakfast. What time is it, anyways? It was noon when I got here. It couldn't be morning all ready could it?"

"It's 3:45 am. Perfect time to have breakfast."

"3:45 am! I should be asleep."

"Well, then, maybe we shouldn't have slept all afternoon," I said as I sat down next to Kalea at the table. When she spilled a tiny droplet of syrup on her chin, I couldn't help it. I leaned over and kissed her. I gently sucked the syrup off her.

She eyed me as I pulled away. "I love you."

"I love you, too," I said as we finished up our waffles.

We spent the next few hours before daybreak snuggling and laughing in bed. I couldn't let her go. I finally had exactly what I had always wanted in the entire world. So, when my alarm went off for me to get ready for work, I was pissed. I didn't want to go to work. I didn't want to leave her for a second.

"I have to get ready for work. You should probably get some more sleep. I have to work until eight tonight because Theo wants all the drywall up and we weren't able to work yesterday," I whispered as I reluctantly pulled away and went to grab a quick shower.

I was sponging myself off when I felt her hands on my back.

"You at least have to let me kiss you goodbye before you go," she said, and then she rained kisses all over me. I didn't want to leave the apartment before. Now the thought of it was killing me.

"I wouldn't have left without saying a proper goodbye. You didn't need to join me in the shower. However, you're always welcome to," I said and captured her lips with mine.

"I hope you have a good day at work. I probably won't be here when you get home tonight. I want to spend some time with my dad."

"I guess that's okay," I said as I gave her a pouty face. I kissed her one last time before I dried off. I really didn't want to go to work. The entire way to the job site I kept thinking about calling Theo to tell him that I wouldn't be there. Kalea probably wouldn't be impressed, though. Even if she loved me, she hated men who just sat around and expected a handout.

⌇

I HAD HAD THE BEST night of my life. I was still dazed from it when I showed up at home. It was my dad's day off, and I was hoping that he and I would be able to do something together. Luck didn't seem to be on my side though. I walked up the path to the front door to find Hannah sitting on the stoop. What in the world was Charles' secretary doing here? I had never liked her. She had always treated me like I was diseased.

"I've been waiting all morning. Where the hell have you been?"

"Umm, well, first off, I don't answer to you, and it's none of your business where I've been. And second, shouldn't you be kissing Charles' ass instead of sitting on my doorstep?"

"Whatever, I came to drop off your divorce papers. You know, you're a real idiot when it comes to guys, Charles is madly in love with you."

"Yeah, because I needed to hear that opinion. Just hand me the papers and get off my property."

"Whatever, whore," she said as she tossed the papers at me and headed off down the driveway. I had no idea when exactly I had first started pissing Hannah off, but it seemed to have been years ago. I didn't understand why Charles kept her on his staff. She was always so grumpy. But, then again, Charles had always kept friends around who either I didn't like or who didn't like me. Not that Charles ever cared anyways. They were his friends. I didn't have to get along with them.

I hadn't even been inside the house for more than five minutes before the phone rang. It was Charles. He wanted to make sure that I got the divorce papers. He also wanted to set up a meeting at his office in about an hour. Reluctantly, I agreed. I thought it would be best to deal with his crap before he ruined more of my day.

I had wanted to spend time with my dad, but it didn't look like that was going to happen. I went upstairs and got changed before I headed out to meet with Charles. I was leaving early, so I figured I would just walk instead of asking my dad for a ride. He was in the living room watching television when I left.

When I got to Charles' office, Hannah was already back. She was sitting at the front desk when I walked in. I wanted to just hand her the papers, but she very rudely insisted that I wait for Charles. I sat in the waiting room for thirty minutes before Charles came out of his meeting.

"Hey, sorry, I'm late. I didn't think the meeting was going to go that long. But then again, you were a bit early anyways. Why don't you just come to my office and we can talk," he said, and then he led me down the winding hallway to where his office was next to Josh's.

"I guess its fine. I could have just left the papers with Hannah, but she made me wait around for you."

"Yeah, I asked her to."

"Well she didn't need to be rude about it. I really don't understand why you keep her around."

"Obligation I guess. Her boyfriend is an idiot at times and doesn't treat her the way that he should. She's always complaining about him."

I placed the signed divorce papers on his desk. "Well, here are the papers. I'm going to go now. I wouldn't want to waste any of your invaluable time."

"We don't have to do this, you know. We could just forget that this little spat ever happened and go back to the way it was. I still love you."

"That doesn't change anything. We're not happy together. There's no point in being in a relationship if it hurts both of us."

"But I still want you, Kalea."

"It's not worth the pain, Charles," I said, and I walked out of his office without looking back. I knew I couldn't be with him. I couldn't live my life the way he expected me to. He would have to learn to live with that.

Hannah beamed as I got onto the elevator. "I guess this is the last time I'll be seeing you around.

"Yeah, now you will have to find someone else to piss off," I said as the doors shut, leaving me with my thoughts.

It was almost three in the afternoon by the time I got home. Dad had left a note saying that he had gone over to his friend's place. He said that he would be home around eight, and that he hoped I had a good day.

He also left a PS on the note saying that Candace had called and she wanted me to call her back. I didn't hesitate. I went to the phone and called her. I had to tell her about Alexi and me, that I didn't exactly know what we were at the moment, but it was heading in the direction of being together.

THE ENTIRE DAY AT WORK was the worst. I kept thinking about Kalea. I couldn't wait until tomorrow so I could see her again. I also wondered what she wanted out of us. Did she expect me to propose now? Or ask her out? Maybe she figured we would only be friends with benefits. Or maybe she hadn't meant it at all.

I didn't want to come across as an idiot and just simply ask her. I wanted it to become clear through the day. However, by the time I was leaving work around eight, I still didn't know the answer. I grabbed a pizza and went to see if Julius wanted to watch the game that was playing that night.

Kalea had said that she had wanted to spend time with her dad, so there was no reason for me to go to her place or home. I missed her already. I wanted to hold her again.

"Julius? What are you up to?" I asked as I entered his apartment. It's a good thing he always left his door unlocked when he was home. I didn't want to go home and smell Kalea all over the place.

"I was just about to sit down and watch the game. I'm guessing you're here to join me and bitch about how much you need Kalea in your life."

"I don't bitch."

"Yeah, you do. You're always talking about how you miss Kalea and how you don't think that the dates you go on with her are actual dates. You've also continuously tell me about how much of an idiot you are for sleeping with her while she was with Charles. I just wish you guys would get a room again so I don't have to hear about it all the time."

I plopped down next to him on the couch. "We did."

"You did what?" he asked and handed me a beer out of the case he had brought into the living room.

"Get a room? We kind of professed our love for one another and, umm, well, ended up naked again."

"What? Great! So, I guess you're not here to bitch about old times. Wait, were you an idiot again? Did you leave her cold, wet and crying saying you didn't want to see her again?"

"No, I didn't do that again. Actually, we spent the night together, and then I went to work this morning with a proper goodbye."

"Awesome!! So, you guys are finally together?"

"I don't really know."

"Now, how in the world does that make any sense? I'm pretty sure you should know whether you're with someone or not."

"Well, usually, yeah. But it's complicated."

"No, it's simple. Isn't that what you're always telling everyone?"

"But this is complicated. I don't know what she wants. I don't know if we're just friends with benefits, dating, or if she wants me to propose. Hell, I don't even know if she wants to be together at all. Maybe she just wants to continue to be friends with me and that's it."

"I doubt she just wants you guys to continue being friends. Didn't you already say that you both professed your love for one another?"

"Well, yeah, but what if she was just saying that because I said it to her?"

"I doubt that's why she said it. Kalea is not the kind of girl that says something she doesn't mean."

"No, she's not. Do you think she wants me to propose to her? Wouldn't that be kind of fast, though?"

"The only way that proposing to her would be fast would be if the two of you didn't count the years you spent as best friends. If you're only counting the time you've been together than it's only been twenty-four hours. That's kind of fast. But you guys have been friends forever, and so I don't think it'd be too fast."

"Is that what I want to do again, though? It didn't exactly work out the first time I proposed to someone."

"That was Drea, a lying skank. This is Kalea we're talking about. Kalea is nothing like Drea. She wouldn't cheat on you."

"She cheated on Charles."

"Yeah, I don't think you're allowed to use that against her, considering the reason you guys are happily together is because you slept with her while she was with Charles. If you hadn't caused her to cheat on him, I doubt that she would have left him. I doubt she would have gone to New Zealand and realized how much she needed you in her life."

"I guess you're right, but—" I was interrupted by a loud knocking at the door.

"I wonder who that could be. Nobody knocks except Kalea."

"She's spending time with her dad tonight," I said as Julius went to the door to open it. I didn't hear him say anything when he got there. He came back and sat down on the couch.

"There you are. I've been trying to reach you all day, Alexi. Where in the world is your cell phone?" My mom said as she came into Julius' living room.

"I guess it's at home, Mom. Why? What's up?" I said as I checked my pockets for my phone. It wasn't there, though. I had probably left it on my nightstand given how preoccupied I was before I left for work.

"Tomorrow is Saturday, you know. We're going out for your sister's birthday. I wanted to tell you that I'll pick you up at 4:30. I want to make sure that you have something nice to wear."

"I have nice things to wear. Thanks for reminding me about Jenna's birthday. I kind of forgot about it, but then I've had a big week."

"Your sister is too important for you to be forgetting about."

"I know, I know. I'm sorry. I'll see you tomorrow at 4:30."

"You better be there, and you better not smell like alcohol," she said as she headed for the door again. I rose to walk her there. She'd raised me to be a gentleman, after all.

"I'll be there and I promise you, my alcoholic days are over. Oh, speaking of which, do you think it would be okay for Kalea to join us for Jenna's dinner?"

"Certainly not! Why in the world would you ask me that?"

"I'm kind of dating her."

"ALEXI COLLIN-HARRIS STARLIN! What in the world are you thinking? You can't date her! She's the reason you were so miserable. I told you to stop hanging out with her. What in the world is wrong with you?"

"Mom, it's not really your choice. It's mine. I love her. I'm not a child anymore. I'm not going to stop being friends with someone simply because you tell me that I shouldn't. I'll see you tomorrow and I won't bring her then."

She was so furious with me that she didn't say anything else before she left. I shook my head and went back to sit on the couch.

"So, I guess that makes up your mind then?"

"What are you talking about?"

"You told your mom that you're dating Kalea. I guess you've decided to ask her out on another date. Or are you going to ask her to be your girlfriend?"

"I guess so," I said. I downed the beer he had given me and pulled out another one. I grabbed a slice of pizza from the box and then offered Julius a slice.

"So much for not being an alcoholic anymore," he chuckled as we settled in to enjoy the game.

"It's not like that. I just don't understand why she thinks that she has a right to tell me who I'm allowed to hang out with or date. It's not like it's her life. It's mine. She already had her chance and she chose my dad."

"Yeah, I think I've only heard her use your full name twice and that's including this time."

"When was the first time you heard her use it?"

"I'm pretty sure we were like ten, and you had broken the vase that she loved that had been her grandmother's because you wouldn't stop throwing your basketball in the house."

"Yeah, that sounds about right. She was really upset about that, after all. She said that I ruined an amazing family heirloom."

THE NEXT MORNING, I WOKE up in my own bed. I checked my cell phone for any sign of Alexi. Sadly though, he hadn't called or texted me all night long. It slightly saddened me to think that he hadn't wanted to talk to me last night. But, then again, he knew I had wanted to spend time with my dad. He was probably just being nice.

Disappointed, I rose from my bed and went to my bathroom. I quickly peeled off my pyjamas and jumped in for a quick shower. It was Saturday. I didn't have anything planned. I missed Alexi, though, so I figured I'd head over to his place to see if we could hang out.

When I was finished my shower and brushed my teeth, I checked my cell phone again. This time there were six text messages, all from Alexi. He did want to see me after all. I dressed and headed downstairs. Alexi texted to say he would be here in an hour.

I had just finished my bowl of cereal when the doorbell rang. Sure enough, it was Alexi, and he was early again. I smiled before I pulled him into my arms for a deep kiss.

"I missed you yesterday. Did you have fun with your dad?" He asked as he shut the door.

I started to put on my shoes. "Actually, I didn't get to hang out with him. Hannah showed up with my divorce papers, and then I had to go meet Charles to give them to him. By the time I got back here my dad had already gone over to his friend's house."

"Oh, so you're officially divorced?"

"Almost. The lawyer needs to look them over, sign the papers and send each of us a certified copy, and then it's all over," I said as we headed back out the door.

"Oh, okay, I see." We got into his car and he drove us over to his place. I wanted to ask him if we were still just friends or if we were more than that, but I didn't want to come across as an idiot.

When we got back to Alexi's apartment, we simply cuddled on the couch and watched a movie. It felt like no time at all had passed before Alexi started getting ready to go out somewhere.

"Do you want me to drive you home?" He asked as he buttoned up a dress shirt.

"I don't really want to go home tonight. Are you going somewhere?"

"Yeah, Jenna's birthday dinner is tonight and my mom will be here in about twenty minutes to pick me up. I'm sorry I didn't tell you before now, but I didn't know how to tell you since my mom doesn't want you to come. Hell, she doesn't even want us to be together."

"What do you mean? She doesn't want us to be friends?"

"Yeah, she doesn't want us being anything. And I really hope that wasn't your way of saying that you only want to be friends. I don't think I could handle that. I love you, Kalea. I want to at least be your boyfriend," he said as he came over and held out his tie for help.

"I love you, too, and nothing would make me happier than being your girlfriend. But what should I do to get your mom to like me again? I don't want you to lose your mom simply because you want to be with me."

"I don't want to lose my mom either, but I can't live without you." He kissed the top of my head as his door-bell rang.

"Am I allowed to just stay here until you get home tonight?"

"Of course, you are. You're allowed here whenever you like. The fridge should be stocked, but if you want a pizza or something there's money in the coffee tin in the cupboard."

"Okay, I love you and I'll see you later," I said as I kissed him goodbye. I watched as he went to his front door and left. So, Linda still hated me. I had to figure out a way to mend the bond between us. Linda and I had always gotten along. But then again, Linda was extremely protective of her only son.

Chapter Seventeen

When I opened the door, I was surprised to see my dad standing there instead of my mom. I guess she was still angry that I wouldn't let her dictate who I could or couldn't hang out with.

"Your mother is extremely mad at you, so she sent me. Speaking of which, how is Kalea anyways?"

"She's good. You're not mad at me for being with her?"

"It was obvious that you two were meant to be together the moment you brought her home when you were twelve," he said. We walked down the steps to his truck.

"I thought that you'd be siding with Mom on this," I said as I climbed into the passenger seat. My dad and I hadn't really gotten along since I was thirteen. I had caught my dad cheating on my mom with some waitress. He claimed he was drunk and when I threatened to tell mom anyways, he slapped me across the face. It had been the first and only time he ever hit me. We hadn't gotten along since. We put up with each other for my mom and my sisters' sake, but we went out of our way to avoid each other.

"How can I? If you're meant to be with her, who am I to judge what's best for you? I still think she should be allowed to come with us, but your mother insists that she stay away."

"Yeah, Jenna loves Kalea; they've always gotten along."

"Yeah, Kalea is part of the family, so what if you and her had an argument, it's not like the entire family argued with Kalea. Family members fight all the time, that doesn't mean you make an outcast of any of them."

"This is Mom we're talking about though. If anyone hurts one of her three angels, as she calls us, she holds a grudge."

"Isn't that the truth?" he said as we pulled into the parking lot of the restaurant. Jenna was standing by the door as we walked up. The second she noticed us, she threw her arms around me. It felt good to see her again. I hadn't seen her in a while.

"I was starting to worry that you two weren't coming at all. Mom is already angry with Sasha. I did not want to be stuck here with her and grandma for the entire time."

"Just grandma? Where's grandpa?" I asked as the three of us went into the restaurant.

"He was in for hip surgery yesterday. They thought he would be out of the hospital in time, but the doctors wanted to keep him another night. It's nothing serious."

"Oh, I see, okay, so why is mom mad at Sash?"

"Do you remember that biker guy that she was dating a few years ago, the one that wouldn't stop hitting her and put her in the hospital, like, ten times?"

"You mean Jake? That wasn't a few years ago, Jenna, that was last year. And yeah, of course I remember him. I wanted his throat cut, but Sash made me promise that I wouldn't go near him." I always kept my promises to my sisters. I loved both of them with my entire being. There wasn't anything I wouldn't do to protect them.

"I can never remember dates, but, yeah, him. She's dating him again, and she's bringing him to dinner tonight. She vows that he wouldn't hurt a hair on her head and that he's not the same person he used to be. But you know Sash, she always looks for the good in people."

"Ah, I can see why mom's not happy with her. I don't think I'm happy with her right now either."

"I know, but please keep it to yourself. It's bad enough that Mom and you, and Mom and Sash are fighting, we don't need more drama. We're supposed to be happy and celebrating my birthday. Oh, and speaking of mom and you, where's Kalea?"

"Kalea isn't coming. Mom hates her right now. I'm sorry, if I would have known you wanted her here, I would have brought her anyways. It's your birthday not Mom's."

"That sucks. I wanted to talk wedding details with her," she said as we finally arrived at the table where mom and grandma were already seated. I grabbed her gently by the arm and swung her face me.

"What do you mean wedding details? I haven't asked Kalea to marry me."

"No silly, Tyson proposed this morning. I want her to be my maid of honour."

"Kalea? You want Kalea to be your maid of honour over Sash or Sierra?"

"Sierra and I aren't getting along. I don't want to choose Sash because she was complaining about how even being just a bridesmaid is so expensive what with the cost of dresses and things. She doesn't want to be my maid of honour. I had to beg her to even be in the bridal party."

"Oh, okay."

Grandma waved me over. "Alexi, come sit, dear. I miss you so much, you're never around anymore."

"Coming Grandma," I called. I looked back at my sister, "Congratulations on the upcoming wedding."

"Thanks, Ix." She threw her arms around my neck again. She had called my Ix since I was born. She was five at the time and couldn't say Alexi, and so it had stuck over the years. It was a lot better than what Sash called me. She usually called me Twerp. She claimed it was because I annoyed her too much growing up.

I moved past my sister to go sit beside grandma. It felt like forever since I had seen her. I gave her a quick hug before I settled into my seat.

"How have you been GG?"

"Oh, I've been good, dear. It's a shame grandpa couldn't be here today. He would have loved to have seen you again."

"I'll swing by to see him next week. I promise."

"Okay, you should bring Kalea. We could all sit and have dinner together."

"Sorry I'm late everyone. Jake was having problems getting his bike to start." Sash said as she joined us at the table with Jake in tow. She had on a long-sleeved black turtleneck, which didn't completely cover the bruises on her neck. So much for him being a changed man. I struggled to control my anger.

"Well, then, you should have found another way to get here on time instead of waiting for the bike to start," Mom said as Sash and Jake took their seats. "And why are you wearing black? It's a birthday not a funeral."

"Just stop, Mom. I'm sure Jenna doesn't want to hear us argue for her birthday." Sasha responded as she glanced around the table.

Thankfully, that's when the waitress came to take our drink order. She also told us that when we were ready we could help ourselves to the buffet. Glad for a distraction, Jenna was the first to jump up and get herself a plate. I simply wanted this dinner to end so that I didn't punch Jake in the face.

Just when I thought I had enough drama to deal with, up at the buffet I spot the last person I want to see: Charles. He was talking and laughing with Josh. I came up behind them and grabbed an empty plate.

"Well, would you look who it is, the wife stealer," Charles snickered as I fell in line.

"Hey, Alexi, shouldn't you be screwing someone else's wife instead of being here?" Josh added as they filled their plates.

"I wouldn't start on him, Josh, he might try to put you through the window." Charles said, and then they took their food and walked away.

Jenna came up beside me. "Ignore them They're idiots. They always have been."

"It's hard to when their idiocy takes up the entire restaurant."

"I know, but we have Jake to worry about. Did you see the bruises that Sash is trying so hard to hide?"

I filled up my plate. "Yeah, I did. I'm trying to ignore the urge I have to cut Jake's throat for laying a hand on Sash as well as ignore those idiots." I shrugged to where Josh and Charles were.

"Well, hopefully everyone eats fast and this can be over as soon as possible."

"It's your birthday, Jenna. It shouldn't be this way."

"No, but it is, and my birthday wish is to spend as little time as possible here. I have my wedding to Tyson to plan anyways. Oh, speaking of which, you should give me Kalea's phone number so we can meet up."

"Or, you could just call my apartment. I'm hoping she'll be moving in soon. I haven't asked her yet, but I was going to tonight."

"All right but we should probably head back to the table. Hopefully everyone still has their head attached."

I laughed and followed after her. It was nice to see her again. I had been so lost in my drunken sorrow over Kalea that I hadn't been the brother that I should have been.

Luckily nothing else happened to destroy Jenna's birthday dinner. Everyone was excited that Jenna was getting married. Jenna asked me over dinner if I would walk her down the aisle. Dad had looked slightly disappointed, but he said that he understood. She had never been close with dad. They were too much alike. Everything always ended in an argument.

When I finally arrived back home, Kalea was asleep on the couch. I tucked the blanket around her and carried her to my bedroom. Although I was extremely careful not to wake her, her eyes opened when I placed her on the soft covers.

"I'm sorry. I didn't mean to wake you. I just thought that it would be more comfortable for you to be in bed instead of on my couch," I said as I kissed her on her cheek.

"I was trying to wait for you. How was dinner?"

"Dinner was all right. Do you remember Jake?"

"You mean the guy that continuously put Sasha in the hospital?"

"Yeah, him. Well Sash is with him again."

"Oh, my goodness. Are you serious? Your mother is probably pissed over that. Maybe she'll forget she hates me."

"Yeah, hopefully," I said as I laughed. I wanted to ask her right then to move in, but I thought she might think it was too soon. I didn't want to have dinners like that without her there. I breathed in her scent as I kissed her. Her eyes fluttered open when I snuck my hand beneath her pajama bottoms to stroke her. She was already soaking wet.

I pulled her pajama bottoms off. I played with her while I kissed her thighs. Her scent made me all the hotter for her. She moaned as I took her in my mouth. I felt her muscles constrict and then relax as I took her over the edge.

I was hard enough to hammer nails as I took off my boxers and drove inside her. I thrusted faster as I felt her climax again. I was blinded again as I felt my own release.

"I love you Alexi." She whispered. I gently pulled myself out, laid beside her and held her close. I never wanted this moment to end.

"I love you too, beautiful." I closed my eyes with a smile on my face.

⁓

I WANTED TO LET ALEXI sleep while I got ready to meet up with Jenna, but he was up instantly when I left his bed. She had called last night to invite me to her favourite cafe for breakfast. I met Alexi's hungry gaze from the doorway to the bathroom as I looked back over my shoulder.

"I figured you'd like to sleep in on your day off," I said. He slipped out of bed and met me in the bathroom. He came up behind me and wrapped his arms around me. His breath scorched my skin as he leaned in to kiss my neck and trail his fingers along my spine. I slowly pulled away, aching for him.

"I have to meet up with your sister. She says that she wants to talk to me about something important."

"I know she does, and I want to talk to you about something important."

"Uh oh, what are you two up to?"

"We're not up to anything together. These are two separate important things. I promise," he said as he turned on the shower. He picked me up and placed me effortlessly in the shower before he joined me.

"I don't have time for this," I said as I tried to leave the shower.

He pulled me closer and kissed me senseless. "Move in with me."

"What?"

"Move in with me. I want you to always be here with me. I want to come home from work to you. I want to be with you, and I don't ever want to be apart."

"Alexi, we can't …"

"Kalea, we can. It's not too fast. We don't have to share the same bedroom if you don't want to. I can clear out the other bedroom if you want. I know you don't want to live at your dad's forever, so why not move in with me?"

"Because your mother hates me. She's not going to let me move in with you. I want to, but I don't think it's the best decision right now."

"If you want to, then you should. Forget about my mom. I'll deal with her. I love you and I want you here," he said as he kissed the top of my head.

"Are we seriously going to do this? Move in together?"

"Of course, we are. Aren't you running late for something?"

"Oh, crap! Yes!" I said. I jumped out of the shower and grabbed a towel. By the time I reached the café, Jenna was almost done her breakfast.

"I'm so sorry I'm late. I got so caught up with Alexi asking me to move in with him that I lost track of the time. I'm sorry."

"It's okay. I figured you might be late because of him. He's always behind schedule for some reason. I think when he was a baby someone cut him open and adjusted his internal clock, and so that's why he's always late."

"Yeah, that would explain it," I laughed and then ordered some waffles from the waiter.

"So, I wanted to have breakfast with you to talk about wedding details."

"Wedding details. Alexi hasn't proposed. Whose wedding are you talking about?" I asked, confused.

"Mine. Tyson proposed yesterday and I spent the day arguing with my sister about being the maid of honour. She doesn't want to be it. She says it's a waste of her time and money. I finally got her to agree to be one of my bridesmaids. I was hoping that because you're like another sister to me, you wouldn't mind being my maid of honour."

"Are you serious? Firstly, congratulations. Second, that really sucks that she won't do that for you. And, of course, I will be. I don't know how well your mom will like that, but I'd love to do that for you," I said and gave her a huge hug. Jenna was getting married. It was so exciting.

"Thank you. I'll deal with my mom. She needs to realize that she's the only one of us that is mad at you. I really wish that you would have been able to come last night—" She was interrupted by her cell phone ringing. She excused herself and went outside to take the call.

Thankfully, that's when my waffles arrived. I slowly picked at them while I waited for Jenna to be done with her phone call. It put butterflies in my stomach to know that I had been chosen to be her maid of honour. Jenna already felt like a sister to me; it was a no-brainer when she asked me.

"Sorry about that. That was Mom. She says she wants to talk to you, and so she's kind of on her way down here right now. You know how she gets when she gets something in her head. I was hoping we could start on wedding stuff, but it looks like that will have to wait," she said and quickly finished up her breakfast. Her eyes drooped when she spotted her mom coming into the café.

Linda took a seat at our table. "There you are. I need to speak with both of you,"

"Hi, Linda, nice to see you again." I beamed from across the table. I already knew she wasn't happy with me; there was no use in acting grumpy over that fact.

She scowled at me as she adjusted herself in the seat. "You're not allowed to move in with him. It's not going to happen. Thomas and I will make sure you don't get the chance."

"My dad? He won't care if I move in with Alexi. I love him and I'm never going to hurt him."

"Yeah, only because you've already done so."

"He hurt me just as much, if not more, than I hurt him. I would never intentionally say or do anything to harm him. Given all the years you've known me, you should know that," I said as I took a gulp of my orange juice.

"Not to mention that it's Alexi's life, Mom. He should be able to do whatever he wants. He's not a baby anymore," Jenna piped in.

"Don't even get into this, Missy," she snapped. "I'm not thrilled that you picked Kalea over Sasha to be your maid of honour, and I have a whole speech ready for you." She glared at Jenna.

"Whatever, I'll let you two speak to each other. I'll go use the restroom," Jenna said, and then she rose from the table and headed off in the direction of the bathroom.

"You're not allowed to move in with Alexi, and you're clearly not allowed to be Jenna's maid of honour. If you move in with Alexi, all you're going to do is hurt him worse. You can't give him what he needs."

"And what exactly is it that Alexi needs, Linda? Does he really need a mother to forbid him to do things and to forbid him from seeing whomever he wants? Is that what he needs in his life?"

"Well, having a mother who cares about him is better than having a cheating whore as a girlfriend."

"I am not a cheating whore, Linda. You know me. I'm not a bad person. If I had told you years ago that Alexi and I were together, you would have been thrilled. What happened?"

"What happened is that you cheated on your husband with my son and then you took off without even a word of goodbye to anyone. We were as close as family could be, and then you just turned your back on everyone. Including Alexi. While he was in a drunken stupor and ruining his life, you were off gallivanting across the world."

"I was studying. I was in university, and I missed him like crazy. I was hurting. Do you know what he said to me when were together?"

"Yes, that he never wanted to see you again."

"Yes, and it hurt. It hurt a lot, and I needed to get over that before I could even think about being with your son. I needed to know that I loved him, and that I wasn't simply looking for a way out of my marriage to Charles. I wanted to be sure that it was real before I took the chance of ruining his happiness. I'm in love with him, Linda, and there's nothing I can do to change that."

"Then why wouldn't you even say goodbye to us?"

"I couldn't. I couldn't stand the thought of you guys hating me for loving your son. But it looks like that happened anyways. I'll see you later. Please ask Jenna to call me," I said before I left. I knew now that she was hurt because I hadn't even told her that I was leaving. Angry that I had ignored her even though she was like a mother to me.

It was a long morning. I simply wanted to go back to Alexi's house and snuggle on the couch watching movies all day long. I still thought it was too soon to move in with one another, but I knew that I wanted to. I needed to think of a way to ask him to wait a bit longer.

Chapter Eighteen

I was doing the dishes up when Kalea returned from breakfast with my sister. She looked a little rattled as she took off her shoes and went to the living room without even a hello. I dried my hands off on the dish towel. Slightly concerned I went into the living room to check up on Kalea.

"Are you all right?" I asked as I sat down on the couch next to her. She had her head in her hands as if breakfast had been a complete disaster.

"I'm fine. I don't want to talk about it," she said without looking up at me.

"You don't seem fine."

"Your mom hates me. I can't move in with you," she said, finally looking up at me.

"I'm sure my mom doesn't hate you. She's just upset right now."

"No, she hates me. She doesn't want me to move in with you, and she doesn't want Jenna to have me as her maid of honour. You have no idea how terrible this feels! I used to have a close relationship with your mom. And now? Now she hates me because of our argument, an argument that hurt me as much as it hurt you." Tears streamed down her face and she put her head in her hands again.

"She doesn't hate you." I said as I pulled her into my arms to hold her. I wanted to make everything better. My anger at my mother increased as she sobbed uncontrollably. "What happened anyways?"

"I was having breakfast with your sister when your mom came in and started saying how I wasn't allowed to move in with you, and how it's awful that Jenna chose me as her maid of honour over Sasha. She hates me, Alexi."

"I'm sorry she said that. I have to go. I'll be back in a little while," I said, my anger overcoming my common sense. My mom was going to get a little piece of my mind. When Kalea was my best friend and nothing more, I hated seeing her cry. Now it tore me to shreds.

I grabbed my sweater and headed outside to my car. I drove the fifteen minutes to my parents' house and walked right in the front door. I found my mother in the garden with her friend Rose.

"Well, hi, sweetie, I was just telling Rose here how you're dating that heartbreaker."

"Mom, she's not a heartbreaker and, Rose, would you please excuse me and mom. I really need to have a conversation with her."

"Why, of course, dear, I'll come back over later. I need to go let Lucy out anyways," Rose said, and then she left the two of us alone.

"Now, why in the world would you send Rose away? She just got here not too long ago."

"That's nice. We need to talk. How dare you tell Kalea that she's not allowed to move in with me? It's my life, not yours. You're the only one who seems to hate her."

"I don't hate her. I just don't want her with you. She cheated on her husband. What makes you think that she won't cheat on you, too?"

"Mom! She's not like that."

"And what is going to happen when she leaves again? You're going to go back to being an unhappy alcoholic, and you won't want to be around anyone. I can't stand back while you ruin your life over a fling."

"Mom, this isn't a fling. I'm in love with her. She's my whole world and I should have seen it earlier. I should have been with her sooner …"

"But you weren't, because subconsciously you knew she was trouble."

"Trouble? Mom! You've known her since we were twelve. You know that's not true. You need to stop this crap. I don't want to hear it anymore. You have a choice to make. Either you accept the fact that I am going to be with Kalea, and you treat her better, or you can say goodbye to me because she's going to be in my life whether you like it or not. It's my life. It's my decision. Choose wisely, Mom." At that I stormed out. I didn't wait for her answer. I was so mad at her.

I loved my mom, but I needed Kalea in my life. If I had learned anything over the past few months, it was that I couldn't live without her. She was my entire life; I didn't want to lose her over my mom's cruelty. I slipped behind the wheel of my car and drove back home.

I DIDN'T KNOW WHERE ALEXI had gone, but I sure hoped it wasn't to talk to his mom. I didn't want him to do anything that he would regret later. I wiped the tears off my face and starting glancing over wedding sites. I didn't know what type of maid of honour Jenna was hoping I would be, but I wanted to make sure I did everything perfectly.

I quickly grew bored of the perfect flowers and beautiful bridal gowns that covered all the wedding sites. I left the computer and was about to put a movie on when my phone rang. I answered on the second ring.

"Hello?"

"Hey, Princess. How's your day?"

"Hi Dad. It's okay, not the greatest day ever, but I'm fine. What's up?"

"Do you still talk to Charles?"

"Uh, no, why?"

"Because he was here a few minutes ago. He said he wanted to tell you something about Alexi. He suggested that Alexi is lying to you."

"He's probably just making stuff up again because he wants to cause havoc. It's probably nothing, Dad."

"He said he was going to try to catch you at Alexi's, and so he's probably on his way over."

"I will deal with him, Dad. He shouldn't be coming over, but I'll make sure he won't bother you again."

"Okay, Princess. I just don't want you to get hurt. Just be careful, all right? You're the only daughter I have. I can't stand to see you heartbroken."

"Okay, Dad. Have a good day. I love you."

"Love you, too, Princess. Goodbye."

Two seconds after I hung up the phone with Dad, Alexi walked through the door. He took off his shoes and gave me a quick kiss before he went into the bedroom. He said he was going to lay down for a bit. I thought about mentioning that Charles might be coming over looking for me, but I thought the better of it. If Alexi came to the door with me, Charles might not say what he came to say. What if Charles was telling the truth? Could Alexi be hiding something from me?

I was going to check on him, but the doorbell rang. It was probably Charles. I would have much rather have gone to see Alexi, but I wanted to know what lies Charles was spewing.

"What do you want?" I asked as I opened the door.

"There you are. I wanted to talk to you. What are you doing here, anyways? I checked your dad's. I checked Julius'. Finally, I had the nerve to check here."

"And what exactly is so important that you had to find me to talk to me about?"

"I cheated on you with Hannah."

"Okay, I guess that's not a surprise. And why does it matter now?" I said, but a slight stab of pain went through my chest. It hurt to know that Charles had cheated on me.

"Because Alexi knew about it. He kept it from you. What else is he hiding?"

"Alexi knew about it? Are you sure? He wouldn't do that. He's my best friend. He wouldn't keep something that significant from me." It may have hurt to think that Charles had cheated on me, but it hurt even worse to think that my best friend had intentionally kept something that important from me. Why hadn't he told me? But then again, what if Charles was lying again?

"Maybe you two aren't as close as you thought you were. I wanted to make sure you knew about it."

"Why would you even bother? It's not like I would ever go out with you again considering you just admitted that you cheated on me. How long were you with her?"

"Four years."

"Four years? Are you kidding me? How in the world could you think that that was all right? And how dare you come after Alexi because he slept with me while we were married. You goddamn hypocrite. I never want to see you again." I slammed the door in his face and turned around to find Alexi standing behind me.

"I'm sorry. I never meant to hurt you."

"Wait a second. You did know?"

"Yeah, I knew. I found out a short while ago. He was on a date with her while I was at a bar. You two were already separated, which I didn't know at the time. Hannah let it slip that she had been dating Charles for the past four years. I didn't want to hurt you, and I knew that it would have hurt you."

"You should have told me."

"You might not have believed me. It was after we had spent the night together in the park, and I was worried you might think it was a story I made up to get you to be with me instead of Charles. I didn't want you to think that I'd ever do something like that."

"Alexi, we've never kept anything from each other. You should have told me whether it would be hurtful or not," I said as I grabbed my shoes and coat.

"Where are you going? We should talk about this."

"I don't want to talk about it anymore. I'm going to my dad's. Clearly, I'm not moving in with you. That would have been a huge mistake."

"Kalea …" I didn't let him stop me. I walked down the stairs, calling my Dad when I reached the bottom. I asked him to come pick me up. He said he would be here as fast as his car would get him here.

I put my head in my hands as I allowed my tears to fall down my cheeks. My heart was shattered: Alexi had not been honest with me. And I was angry, too, that I'd been too stupid to see that Charles had cheated on me for so long.

However, I felt angrier at Alexi for not telling me the truth when he found out. He had a point, though; I probably would have thought that he was simply trying to get me to leave Charles.

I had been still hurting from what Alexi had told me after our night in the park that I might not have listened to him anyways. I had been terrified of talking to him because his declaration of not ever wanting to see me again. My anger slightly subsided as I thought about what Alexi had said.

Thankfully, I didn't have to wait long before my dad pulled into the driveway. I climbed into the passenger seat, and we took off towards home. Thankfully my dad sensed that I didn't want to talk about it. I closed my eyes as I tried to think about a way to handle the entire thing.

Should I be angry at Charles, Alexi, or myself? Conflicting emotions played themselves out in my head even after I had gone to bed for the night. I started classes at my new university tomorrow and I needed to get to sleep, but it didn't seem like that was going to happen.

Why did Charles have to bring up the past? It's not like this just happened. But, then again, it did just happen for me.

Chapter Nineteen

I wanted to go after her. I wanted to make her understand. I knew she was hurting, and I knew that I was one of the reasons why, but I still felt I did the right thing. I figured I would give her the night to think over what had happened, and then I would go talk to her in the morning.

I set my alarm for earlier that usual because though I wanted to go talk to Kalea, I also didn't want to be late for work. I made sure to give myself an hour to speak with Kalea.

Before long I was driving up her winding driveway, grocery-store flowers beside me. When we were growing up, my mom always said that when a man brought a woman flowers when she was mad at him, he was more likely to be forgiven. I didn't know if any of that was true, but I wanted all the luck I could get.

Luckily, the store had some lilies. Lilies were Kalea's favourite, and I was hoping she would be excited to receive them. I parked my car, gathered my courage, and walked up to the front door. I knew it was early, but Kalea's dad would be leaving for work soon, so they should be up. Or at the very least he should be up.

I knocked on the door and waited. Within minutes Kalea's dad opened the door.

"Hello, Mr. Conwell. How is your morning going?"

"Alexi, what in the world are you doing here at this hour? Kalea is not even out of bed yet."

"I know, sir, but I really need to talk to her before I go to work. I can't leave things the way I did yesterday. I need to fix it."

"Fix it? You refused to tell her that the man she was marrying was dating another woman. You were her man of honour. That was your job. You were responsible for making sure that Kalea wasn't making a mistake with her life. You sat back and allowed her to marry him, even though you knew that she'd get hurt from it."

"I didn't actually know at the time of the wedding, sir. I only found out afterwards. If I had known at the wedding. I would have said something, and she never would have married him."

"Whatever. I have to get to work. You're walking a thin rope, though. That's my baby girl's heart you're playing with, and if she ends up even the slightest bit more hurt, I'll see to it that you never please another girlfriend in your life." He then grabbed his coat and walked out to his car.

Even though Kalea was still in bed, I went upstairs. I had been in her room numerous times before, and I figured I'd be allowed in now. I slowly opened the door and quietly walked up to her bed where she was sleeping, her hair spread over her pillow.

I couldn't decide whether I should wake her, or just leave a note along with the lilies on the pillow beside her. I wanted to talk to her, though. However, she would probably be happier if I just left them on her pillow.

I gently placed the lilies on her other pillow and went to grab a piece of paper and pen from her desk. When I opened her desk drawer, Kalea's eyes flew open.

"What are you doing here?" she asked groggily rolling over. She immediately noticed the lilies. "Oh, my goodness, they're gorgeous."

"I was hoping you'd like them," I said and sat on the edge of her bed.

"I'm still mad at you. I know you only brought these because of that saying of your mom's."

"That's why I'm here. I want to talk you about what happened."

"You should have told me."

"You wouldn't have listened. You were in New Zealand, for crying out loud, and I didn't even know you had left."

"I didn't tell you that because you specifically said you never wanted to see me again."

"You know I didn't mean that. I was angry with myself for allowing that to happen. Don't get me wrong. I love you, and I loved you that night, but it was wrong to sleep with you while you were married."

"Well, that's why I didn't tell you about New Zealand. I couldn't talk to you then."

"And that's the same reason why I didn't tell you about Charles and Hannah. It's like there was a wall between us that never used to be there because of what happened. I didn't want to hurt you, and then I found out from Julius that you weren't even with Charles anymore, and so I didn't think it mattered. You were done with him anyways."

"I guess it doesn't matter anymore, but it still hurts. You kept something from me that you should have immediately told me."

"I know I did, and I'm sorry."

"Whatever. Shouldn't you be going to work?"

"Yeah, but this is more important to me than work."

"It shouldn't be. Theo is going to fire you. You haven't exactly been the greatest employee lately."

"All right. Fine. I'll go to work, but this conversation isn't over until you forgive me," I said as I left her room. I went downstairs and out to my car to head to work. I wanted to stay and beg her to forgive me, but I knew she was right. I needed to go to work. I had bills to pay, and I needed to a job to do that.

I was almost at the jobsite when Theo called me. The other guys hadn't finished what they were supposed to on the house, and so he didn't need me that day. I wanted to turn around and go back to Kalea's house, but I figured that I would go see Julius instead. It had been a while since I had hung out with him, and Kalea probably wasn't ready to forgive me.

I was almost to Julius' house when I remembered that it was a Tuesday. Julius would have already left for work. That left me with only two options: either I head back to see Kalea, or I go home. I didn't really want to go home without Kalea, but I also knew that she wasn't ready to forgive me yet.

Why hadn't I just told her? None of this crap would be happening now if I had simply called her when she was in New Zealand. If only I could change that. But, then again, if life worked that way, I would already be married to Kalea. That's what I wanted. I wanted to be her husband. I wanted to spend the rest of my life with her. It was too soon though. Wasn't it?

She'd never agree to marry me yet. We had just started dating, and she wasn't comfortable moving in with me. But I couldn't lose her. It was all or nothing; I had to take a chance. Plans swirled around in my head about how I would ask her.

I was at home on the couch writing up ideas when a knock at my door startled me. Who would be here now? Only Theo knew I had the day off. I slowly rose from the couch and opened the door. The last person that I wanted to deal with was my mother, and there she was.

"Alexi, I need to talk to you about this ultimatum of yours."

"Mom, I don't want to talk about it. You either accept Kalea or you lose me; it's not difficult. Especially since you are the only one in our family who seems to hate her."

"Well, that's cause no one else seems to care about who hurts you."

"No, no one else holds a grudge against someone over an argument."

"You were becoming an alcoholic, Alexi! I can't just allow her back in your life to let you become that again."

"Mom, that's just it. I was only an alcoholic when she was gone. When she's here everything in my life seems right. She makes my life better, and I can't live without her. I need her in my life."

"Alexi—"

"—No, I don't want to talk about it anymore. I'm going to ask her to marry me. Now, you're either going to be in my life or not. The choice is yours," I said as I gently closed the door. I knew she would get mad at me for that, but I had more happy things to think about, like how to propose to Kalea.

I COULDN'T BELIEVE THAT MY own son was making me choose between accepting the girl who broke his heart and living without him. I couldn't live without my son, but I wasn't ready to forgive Kalea either.

I didn't know what to do. I had to go home and talk with Curtis. He usually knew exactly what to do in these types of situations. He always thought of the pros and cons of every situation.

I drove out of Alexi's parking lot and back home. Curtis was off work today, and I was hoping he hadn't left for his canoe trip. He had planned to go canoeing over the next two days with his brother Joe.

Luckily, when I got home, he was still loading up the car.

"Hey, Sweetheart. Where did you go?"

"I had to go speak with Alexi about the ultimatum he gave me."

"Oh, yeah? Did you win this time?"

"No, I didn't. He claims that Kalea is the one who makes his life better. He says he's going to ask her to marry him."

"Good for him. It's about time they were together for real. They've been closer than white on rice for years. You know this already though. She was like a daughter to us. We've always accepted her. What's made you change your mind this time?"

"She hurt him, Curtis. She hurt my baby. That's not something that's easy to forgive."

"Do you remember when they decided to rearrange all the furniture in Alexi's bedroom when they were fourteen?"

"Yeah, I do, she dropped that old antique desk on his foot. He had to wear a cast for three months and use crutches."

"You forgave her for that. And how about the time down at the cottage when we were playing baseball?"

"Oh, yes, the concussion he had from that bat hitting him. She should have known not to throw the bat after she hit the ball with it. He was in pain for six months."

"And, again, you forgave her for that, too. How is this any different?"

"She broke his heart."

"And it seems like his heart is what she's healing. She loves him, and he loves her. We've always known that they would get married. It was simply a question of when. So, stop fighting it. Just forgive her like you have all those other times. And another thing, what made him stop drinking?"

"He stopped drinking when Kalea came home. Are you trying to say that she's the reason that he isn't an alcoholic anymore?"

"That's exactly what I'm trying to tell you. Anyways, I should go pick up Joe for our canoe trip. I love you, and I'll see you in a couple of days," he said, and then he climbed into his truck and pulled out of the driveway.

I didn't want to forgive her. The baseball incident and the desk incident were accidents that could have happened to anybody, but she intentionally left him. She purposely caused him pain and caused him to start drinking.

I knew, though, that there was no other way to be in my son's life. I might as well get used to her. I wouldn't be nice to her for a while, I decided, and it would take a long time to get back to where we used to be, but I would give her a second chance. Not for me but for Alexi. I couldn't bear the thought of losing my only son.

⁓

My first day at the University of Western Ontario was difficult. I didn't know where anything was, and it seemed like the campus stretched on forever. Luckily, my dad picked me up from class after my first day.

"How was your day, Princess?" he asked when I climbed into the passenger seat.

I closed my eyes and slumped back against the seat. "It was long, and I kept getting lost. This campus is so big, I don't think I'll ever get the hang of it."

"What about your classes?"

"They're okay. I had Literary Authors and Narrative Theory today. Tomorrow I have Romance across the Ages, Narrative Theory, and Ancient Epics. I can't wait for Romance across the Ages. It should be a good course."

"Sounds like tomorrow is going to be packed."

"It is. I'm exhausted, but I have a report to start tonight. I don't want to fall behind."

"Well, dinner is already ready. I made Shepard's pie when I got home from work."

"Awesome, I can eat and then get right to work."

"Are you going to think about what happened between you and Alexi? Maybe call him and talk to him about it?"

"I hope not. I don't want to talk to him about it. My mind will probably make me think about it, though. I just wish he had told me. We've never kept anything from each other before."

"Yes, but would you have really wanted him to tell you about Charles and Hannah? Would you have listened?"

"No, I probably wouldn't have listened. But I don't know how I would feel if Alexi had told me."

"Okay, we'll try this another way. If Alexi were cheating on you, and Julius told you, how would you feel?"

"I would be very angry with both Julius and Alexi. I would be mad at Julius for not minding his own business. He shouldn't be poking his nose in mine and Alexi's business … Oh, I get it."

"It was a mistake not to tell you, but it also would have been a mistake to tell you, Princess. Everyone makes mistakes. All we can do is look past their mistakes."

"Thanks, Dad."

"So, are you going to call Alexi?"

"Not tonight, maybe tomorrow," I said as we reached dad's house. Even though I had grown up here, this house didn't feel like it belonged to me anymore. The only place that did was Alexi's apartment. Even though we hadn't been together long, I guess Alexi was right, I should move in with him.

I was thinking about calling him before I ate, but my phone rang. It was Candace.

"Hello?"

"Hey, you. I haven't talked to you in what seems like forever. How are things with you and Alexi? Have they heated up yet?"

"Where in the world do you come up with the things you say? Heated up yet? Seriously? That's what you want to say?"

"Well, have you two pulled your heads out of the sand yet?"

"It's a good thing I know what you're asking, nobody else would, that's for sure. We were together, but then something big happened, and I'm kind of mad at him. I was just thinking about forgiving him, but then you called."

"Oh, my goodness, what ruined it this time? What's this something big you're talking about?"

"Well, I found out that Charles was cheating on me. He had this four-year relationship with his secretary Hannah—"

"—The bitch that hated you? Well, I guess we now know why. So, what does this have to do with your man?"

"If you would let me finish, maybe I could tell you."

"Fine, I won't interrupt again."

"Anyways, when I was in New Zealand before Alexi even knew I was there, Alexi was in a bar and he saw Charles and Hannah together, and they let it slip that they'd been together for four years. Anyways, so Alexi was put in the drunk-tank for putting Charles in the hospital. He knew about them being together, and he didn't tell me. If he kept something that big from me, what else could he be hiding?"

"Oh, girl, you're being silly. Alexi only hid that from you because he knew it would hurt you. He went to jail for beating the crap out of Charles, for crying out loud. It's not like he was condoning Charles' cheating."

"I am not saying that. I wasn't with Charles anymore when Alexi found out. I was in New Zealand with you."

"See! Exactly. What's the point in telling you something that doesn't even affect you anymore? Call him, tell you love him and you're sorry for being brainless. He'll forgive you, he's madly in love with you."

"I have a report to do. I shouldn't be calling anyone."

"Well, whatever. I will let you get back to your report. I have to get back to sleep anyways. Love you, Girly."

"Love you, too," I said and hung up. I decided to work on my report some and then have dinner. I wanted dinner to be a reward for doing my homework. I started in on it, and my mind went blank. I wanted to be at home. I didn't want to be at my dad's.

I would have to talk to Alexi tomorrow to see if he could forgive me. I wanted to be with him. I wanted to move in with him. I didn't want to be like his mom and hold a grudge against him. I still needed to figure out a way to get his mom to forgive me, but that could wait.

Chapter Twenty

"Hey, Julius, it's me," I called as I walked into Julius' apartment.

"I'm in the kitchen. I was just making dinner. I have an extra steak if you'd like."

"Sure, that'd be cool. I came over here to talk to you. I want to ask Kalea to marry me," I said. I heard something shatter.

"Are you serious? Already?"

"Already? We waited forever to actually be together," I said. I came into the kitchen to find Julius sweeping up broken glass from the plate he had dropped.

"I guess so. How are you going to do it?"

"That's just it. I can think of a million ways, but it doesn't seem to be enough. I was hoping you'd be able to help me."

"Help you plan a marriage proposal?"

"Exactly."

"And how would you like me to help, Prince Charming?" he said as he went back to fixing dinner.

"Well, I have a list of things that I've put together to do, but I can't decide which ones to use. I know that I want to get her flowers, lilies to be exact, with an apology card."

"Why would you need an apology card?"

"Because I didn't tell her that Charles had been cheating on her with Hannah for four years." Julius lost his grip on yet another plate, and it shattered against the tile.

"You have got to stop throwing out bombshells when I'm cooking dinner. We're not going to have any plates left to eat off."

"I'll clean it," I said as I grabbed the broom and dustpan.

"So why didn't you tell her?"

"Because I found out when she was already in New Zealand. She'd already left him. I had to spend the night in the drunk tank for punching his lights out."

"Okay, so, yes, you need the apology card. You should have told her."

"And hurt her? I should have told her something that had nothing to do with her anymore simply to hurt her?"

"Okay, I guess not, but you still need the apology card. What else were you thinking of?"

"I was thinking about a giant stuffed animal, a box of chocolates and, obviously, a ring."

"Yeah, keep the ring. I wouldn't go for a giant, stuffed animal though. Something small—a stuffed puppy, penguin, or kitten."

"Penguin?"

"Yeah, women always like penguins."

"Okay, so we have a bouquet of lilies, a stuffed penguin, a ring and an apology card. Where should I ask her?"

"I don't know. Where is she tomorrow?"

"In class. She's in class tomorrow."

"Okay, so why don't you ask her during lunch or something? She probably wouldn't like if you asked her in front of one her classes."

"She might not like being the centre of attention, but that's the perfect place to ask her. It's a public declaration of my love for her."

"Well, then, if that's what you're going to do, you're going to have to find out what classes she has tomorrow and figure out which one to propose to her in."

"Yeah, maybe she has a Romantic Literature course tomorrow or something like that, that would work."

"Wait a minute, what about the ring? How are you going to afford a ring?"

"Oh, I already have the ring. I inherited my grandma's ring when she and grandpa got new ones. It's beautiful, and Kalea's always loved it."

"Oh, that's right, I forgot about that. So, what are you going to wear?"

"What do you mean, what am I going to wear? Can't I just wear anything?"

"You want to show up with ripped jeans and a rocker T-shirt to ask the girl of your dreams to marry you? Are you serious?"

"I guess not. No, I wouldn't want to do that."

"Dinner's ready. You want to watch the game as we eat and discuss this some more."

"Yeah. I don't think I have anything suitable to wear."

"Well, depending on what time her class is tomorrow we can go shopping in the morning to grab something for you to wear."

"Yeah, I'm not going to work tomorrow. I'm going to call in sick."

"I guess I will too then; that way I can help you."

"Thanks."

"Kalea and Alexi, the wedding of the century. Two love-birds meant to be together since they were twelve-years-old finally getting hitched. That's all everyone will talk about."

"Oh, yeah, and what do you get out of this?"

"I get to be there for history in the making." I shook my head and laughed at his logic. I was really going to do this. I was going to ask Kalea to marry me. I really hoped she didn't say no. That would be a complete let down, and it would ruin me from proposing to anyone ever again.

———o

My first class was Narrative Theory, and it seemed to take forever before it was finally over. Immediately after Narrative Theory I had Ancient Epics. Ancient Epics went by quickly; it was a very entertaining course. I had a two-hour break between Ancient Epics and Romance Across the Ages.

Jenna was meeting me for lunch so that we could start on some of the wedding details. She was planning her wedding for ten months away, but it felt like it was coming up fast.

"There you are. I was hoping I wouldn't have to run all over in search of you," she called as she ran up to me.

"Yeah, I was hoping I wouldn't get lost trying to meet you. Let's head to the food court. I have to eat while we meet because Romance across the Ages is three hours long without any breaks."

"Then, yeah, Alexi would kill me if I caused you to miss lunch. He's always saying how you never eat enough anyways."

Luckily, the food court was one of the places that I knew how to get to. They had a lovely little sandwich place mixed in with all the other fast-food type restaurants. It was quaint and served homemade salads, soups and sandwiches. We decided, well, I decided, that's where we should go for lunch.

"So, what colours were you and Tyson thinking of for your wedding? Do you have a colour you want for the bridesmaids' dresses? Because we could start looking at flowers for the bouquets."

"Yeah, actually. I wanted the girls in a bright purple. I was hoping to have two different shades of pink in their bouquets. I figured I might as well go really girly after all."

"That sounds awesome. Okay, do you have any specific flowers that you want in the arrangements? Like roses? Carnations? Lilies?"

"I haven't really thought that far ahead yet, but I hate roses unless they're yellow, and that doesn't fit with the other colours I like. Carnations are pretty, but aren't they always used in weddings? I want something different."

"Okay, how about cherry blossoms and azaleas? We could find another dark-pink flower to go in the mix, too, and we should probably either do a lavender flower or a white one."

"I like cherry blossoms. They're so pretty. I don't know what azaleas look like and, yeah, if we are going to do another colour of flower, I would want to go with white, not lavender."

I opened a word document with my laptop and started documenting everything. "Okay, so cherry blossoms are in. How about begonias in white or pink or hydrangeas in pink?"

"Maybe we could go with the hydrangeas in pink and find a tiny, white flower to dispense through the bouquet. What about clematis? They're like a light-pink with white in them already. Could we use those?"

"Jenna, it's your wedding. We can use whatever type of flower you want," I laughed as I typed it all down.

"I guess so, but it has to look nice."

"True, but all the flowers you mentioned go well together, and so it's fine. So, who all is in the bridal party?"

"Well there's you as my maid of honour. Sash as my honoured bridesmaid, and then there's Sierra, Kristin and Molly as my bridesmaids. On Tyson's side, there's Marcus who is Tyson's best man, then Spencer, Ronny, Alexi and Drew—they're his groomsmen. I haven't chosen the flower girl or ring bearer yet. It's going to be hard, though, because it's all little boys on my side of the family and on Tyson's side there's the triplets. How do you choose with triplets?"

"You don't choose one with triplets; you just have three flower girls. They will look really cute walking down the aisle either together or single file." I laughed at the absurd idea of choosing between triplets. That was simply asking for a sibling war.

"Yeah, I guess so. Oh, my goodness, you should be getting to class. I'm so sorry I stopped you from finishing your food. Alexi's going to kill me."

"Don't worry about it. I'll finish in class. We're allowed to have food in class provided we don't leave the class to go get it."

"Okay, thank you for the help. The girls want to get together next week to go dress shopping. I figured it would be better if we tried to kill two birds with one stone, so to speak, and I booked all of you in for appointments for bridesmaid's dresses, and then myself in a bridal appointment right before. If all of us can get our dresses, it will be one less thing we'll have to worry about."

"That sounds like a great idea. Message or call me with the details. I have to run. I'll see you next week, Jenna," I said as I rose from our table to leave.

"Have fun in class," she said and then waved. I literally ran to class. I didn't want to be late. I hadn't been to this class yet, and I didn't want to have to walk in during the middle of class. I hated doing anything that brought attention to myself.

I thought I saw Julius as I was headed to class, but I shook myself, saying that it was only my imagination. What would he be doing on campus? He had no reason to be here. He should be at work.

I found a seat in the middle of the classroom amid the sea of bodies so I would be less likely to be called on. I knew my romance literature well, but I wasn't ready to speak in front of the class.

The teacher, Mrs. Ketler, left for a bathroom break about two hours into the class. That's when the song "Marry Me Today" started playing from the back of the classroom. A gentleman walked in, wearing a suit, sunglasses and a top hat. He was carrying a bouquet of lilies and a stuffed beagle puppy.

It took me a moment to realize that the man standing at the front of the classroom was Alexi. He looked straight at me as he removed his sunglasses and placed his hat on the teacher's desk. He walked to where I was staring dumbfounded at him.

His smile reached his ears as he handed me the flowers and the puppy. The lilies had a card attached with a small message that read: I'm sorry. He pulled a small box out of his pocket, and then he got down on one knee. He opened the box to reveal his grandmother's ring. I couldn't believe what I was seeing. This couldn't be happening, I thought, as I felt my cheeks redden. I was in the middle of a class. He couldn't be doing this now.

"Kalea, you are my entire world. Without you I am a shadow of the man I wish to be. With you, everything is better. Everything is perfect. I know it hasn't been long, but it feels like it's been forever. I love you, and I want you to spend the rest of your life with me. Nothing would make me happier than if you agreed to be my wife. Will you marry me?"

The entire class held its breath waiting for me to answer. My cheeks were as red as tomatoes in the sunshine, and I wanted to shrink to the size of an ant. I took a deep breath before I answered quietly: "Yes, I'll marry you."

He quickly placed the ring on my finger and pulled me into his arms. The entire class let out a round of applause. A loud cough from the front of the room brought us back to reality. Mrs. Ketler had returned from the washroom.

"I hate to burst in on that perfectly-placed proposal, but I do have a class to finish teaching. If you'd just take a seat beside your wife-to-be, I can get on with it."

"Sorry, Mrs. Ketler," Alexi apologized as he sat down in the seat next to mine.

"Now, where were we? Oh yes, the romance of Romeo and Juliet ..." I couldn't focus on the rest of the lesson. Alexi had asked me to marry him. I felt like everything was falling into place.

I COULDN'T WAIT UNTIL KALEA'S class was over. I looked over to where Julius was hidden in the back of the classroom with a tiny boom-box. He smiled as he saw me look at him. It had been a great idea for him to be in the class so he could play the right song. The entire thing went better than expected.

I had held my breath the entire time I waited for her to answer. I thought that she was going to say 'no.' Then again, I had to remember that Kalea was shy. She never liked speaking in public, especially when all the attention was on her.

I had never really liked the story of Romeo and Juliet, but I dealt with it anyways. It was just one class. I could handle it. Luckily, the teacher didn't pick me out of the class. When I had gone to Kalea's classes before, her teachers always picked on me because I wasn't in the class.

When class was finally finished, I walked Kalea to her locker and then out to my car. I had already told her dad what I was planning on doing so he wouldn't try to pick her up from class.

"Would you like to go out for dinner? Or maybe grab something to take out?"

"How about dinner and a movie? That new comedy just came out, and it should still be in theatres."

"You're sure that you want to spend the evening of the day you became engaged at a cramped movie theatre?"

"Well, no, I guess not. Let's go out for dinner and then we can go home … or well back to your place."

"Deal. But it's your place, too, now, you know. You can call it home. Where would you like to go for dinner?"

"How about Gigi's? I haven't been there since we went together."

"Yeah, we can go there," I said as I thought back to the last time we were there. Kalea had been wearing this red cowl-neck blouse and her hair had been done in bouncy curls. She hair was curled today, but it was pulled back into a ponytail. She was wearing a green tank-top with a lemon-yellow sweater over top.

She looked amazing as ever. I told her to wait while I opened the door for her. I helped her out of the car, and then walked her to the restaurant. We were immediately seated in a romantic booth. I made sure to order champagne with our meal to celebrate.

"You really shocked me today," she said as she put down her menu.

"Oh, yeah, and why is that?"

"Isn't it too early for us to be engaged?"

"Are you happy with it?"

"Well, of course. I would never had said 'yes' if I didn't want to marry you." She paused our conversation so the waitress could take our order. This time we both got the lasagna.

"I'm really glad you said yes. I love you."

"I love you too, Alexi."

We finished off our dinner, and we stayed a little longer, enjoying each other's company. When we did leave, we went straight home. We went straight upstairs. It was late when we got home.

"I'm really tired. I should probably just go to bed. I have class tomorrow, and you have to go to work tomorrow."

"I'll join you. I have to be up early for work," I said as I kissed her. I wanted to do more than kiss her, but I knew she was right. I knew I should just go to bed and go to sleep.

"Okay, we should feed Moses first, though."

"Yes, we should," I said as I quickly filled Moses dishes and followed her to the bedroom. I stripped down to my boxer shorts, and I pulled her against me.

"I love you, beautiful." My lips found hers in the darkness. I knew I should have been letting her get to sleep, but I wanted her so badly.

"I love you too." She said as she put her arms around my shoulders. I nuzzled her neck while my hands slipped her tank top off. I suckled her newly exposed breasts and circled my tongue around her nipples.

Her hands slipped beneath my boxers and stroked me. I could feel the blood pulsing where her hand was and I couldn't take it any longer. I yanked my boxers off and gently pulled her pajama bottoms off.

I noticed how wet she was when I stroked her with my fingertips. I kissed her before I drove myself into her wetness.

It took all my control not to finish right there. Her hands clutched at my back as her moans deepened.

"Look at me Kalea," I said. I quickened my thrusts and her eyes widened. They glazed over and I finally let myself go.

It was one of the best moments of my life. I needed her in my life, and I had her. She had agreed to be my wife. I was never going to let her go again. I drifted peacefully off to sleep with Kalea naked in my arms.

I WOKE UP WITH THE greatest sensation in the world. I had arms wrapped around me tight, and Alexi was breathing on my neck. I didn't want to move. I wished I could stay in this one perfect moment forever.

Just as I thought I would get my wish, the alarm went off. Alexi nearly shot through the ceiling. I heard Moses pawing at the door. I groaned and then rolled over to snuggle into Alexi.

"I wish I could snuggle, but I have to go to work, and you have class this morning."

"I know, but I'm perfectly happy right where I am," I said as I wrapped my arms tighter around him and pulled his lips to mine for a kiss.

"Theo will kill me if I don't show up today. I already called in sick yesterday so I could ask you to marry me. Theo wasn't too pleased that I wasn't showing up yesterday. If I call in sick again today, he will fire me."

"But then you'd be home all the time. I think I'm okay with that," I teased as I held him tighter.

"Sure, but then we wouldn't have enough money to have this apartment. We would have to move into your dad's place.

As much as I like your father, I don't think he wants us intruding on the Conwell Mansion."

"I guess so," I said and laughed at the absurd nickname Alexi had given my house when we were younger. Reluctantly, I let him go.

We were both almost ready to leave when the doorbell rang. It was still early in the day. Who in the world would be coming over to visit at this hour?

Chapter Twenty-One

I got dressed as fast as I could. I heard Alexi get into the shower as I opened the door. It was Linda. I didn't know what to say or do, and so I simply smiled and hid my ringed finger behind me.

"Hey, Linda. It's nice to see you. Alexi just went into the shower, but he shouldn't be too long."

"That's all right. I'm not here to speak with him. I'd rather speak with you, if that's okay."

"Sure, come on in," I said as I gestured towards the living room. "Would you like some coffee or something else to drink?"

"No, I'm fine, but I want to talk to you. I've forgiven you a lot. You have caused my son pain, over and over again. You dropped a desk on his foot; you hit him in the head with a baseball bat. I hadn't really thought of those things until Curtis mentioned them to me. He's my only son, Kalea. I don't want to lose him."

"I'm not going to hurt him. I'm in love with him, Linda."

"I know. You are destined for each other. I need time, though. I need time to forgive you. I can't do it right away."

"I ..."

"Let me finish, please. You seem to be the one that can heal him. The one that can make him feel better when he is at his lowest. I want you to make him happy. I want you to give him everything. If you can do that, if you can make him happy for the rest of his life, I can forgive you," she said as I heard the shower turn off.

"Who was at the door?" Alexi asked as he came out of the shower wearing only a towel. "Mom! What are you doing here? I told you, I don't want you in my life if you can't accept Kalea."

"That's what I'm here to talk about. She makes you happy. She helps heal you. All I want for you is to be happy. I want to be in your life. I need to be in your life. If Kalea can promise to always make you happy, I can eventually forgive her," she said as she stood up to leave.

"Thank you, Mom. I guess there is something that Kalea and I need to tell you then."

"You're engaged."

Alexi looked at me.

"How did you know that? I swear, Alexi, I didn't tell her," I said

"No, she didn't tell me. I saw her ring, even though she tried to hide it. It looks good on her. I had better leave, though. I'll call you tomorrow," she said as she headed to the door. "Oh, and congratulations."

I watched as the door closed behind her. Alexi wrapped his arms around me.

"I think I'm going to call in, anyways. I want to spend the day with you," he said as he picked me up and carried me into the bedroom. He set me down and looked in my eyes.

"I love you, Alexi, and I plan on making you the happiest man in the galaxy."

"You already have, Kalea. Just you being here, with me, makes me that happy."

The End